Livin' &

Lovin'

in

Texas

by

SJ Banham

Acknowledgements
Writing a book of any kind takes more than just the author to make it real. Therefore, thanks go to: Robert and Chloe, for giving me the space to write it. My beta readers Jo, Karen, Lynda and Chloe for your time, enthusiasm, and feedback. Helen Baggott for your editing services and Jessica Bell for designing the cover.

For Robert and Chloe

Chapter One

The sun's delicate blush illuminated all it touched as Garrett Cobb buckled his jeans, pulled on his boots, and adjusted his Stetson.

The first night back home from any trip was always spent under the stars, not in the restrictive confines of a bedroom. Travelling had its fun side but at times it was wearying and arduous. He somehow felt older, more mature and ready to settle. If he hadn't seen what the rest of the world was like, how else could he grow as a man or make life decisions?

He'd spent half a year seeing all the world he planned to see, from watching the sun set behind Notre Dame cathedral to feeling the rain fall on his face outside Buckingham Palace. Now home, he was satisfied nothing could beat the fiery Texan heat, nor the thrill of herding steer, constructing buildings, and living life under the Lone Star flag.

Returning to his beloved Maynard gave him a base while he worked out his next move, and now he was huddled in her warm bosom, her loving embrace, it made him wonder why he ever wanted to stray in the first place.

Then Billy's face crept into his head. The boy was a handful, he was just that kind of kid and now in his twenties, it was clear he still needed guidance. As the good big brother his mother had raised him to be, Garrett stepped up to the challenge, because as sure as hell Hank wasn't up to any more fathering.

Yeah, he reminded himself, *that's the reason I left. That's the reason right there.*

Garrett turned over his cot-roll, tied it in place and threw it in the back of his truck. He turned the key, listening to the engine sing its own Morning Chorus and as the wheels threw up dust, it coated his throat.

He needed coffee in a bad way. And a bagel. Just like the ones Meg made at the diner; hot, hard and soft all at once. He'd never tasted a bagel until he'd tasted one cooked by Megan Meyer. The girl had magic fingers. A tingle in his tummy took his breath away as he remembered exactly how magic those fingers had been once upon a time. They'd brought him as close to heaven as a man ever hoped to get.

Damn Meg for being so fine. Damn her more for straying. Billy and his mischievous charm had a knack of ruining everything Garrett ever worked for: the family, relationships, life. For Billy, Meg was just another conquest. He didn't love her like Garrett did, enough to seal the deal with a proposal.

Garrett drove to the diner and waited in the parking lot. It was still early; tradespeople went about their business transferring boxes from the backs of trucks to carts then walking them into their destinations. Garbage truck engines roared in intervals as men collected bins filled with waste from the backs of buildings. Gulls and crows swooped from the sky to the street in seconds, each eager for that piece of bread and last night's discarded burger. Fighting like the Cobb brothers over Meg.

It reminded him of the day he left, sitting there in his truck with all the world's decisions resting on his twenty-eight-year-old shoulders. He remembered it in detail: His flight was booked, his cases were packed, and his passport was nestled in his top pocket, along with the ring.

Inside the diner, Meg was serving Billy. That was his first hurdle.

"Coffee, bro?" Billy said. "Meg's made a fresh pot."

"Sure." Garrett took a seat the opposite end of the counter and placed his Stetson on top. It was well past breakfast, but everything cooked by Meg's hand was worth eating at any time of day. Even the aromas wafting out from the back of the kitchen were good enough to make a grown man weep.

"How come you ain't gone yet?" Billy gulped coffee to ease the journey of a fresh bite of waffle. His big brown eyes distracted attention from his apparent lack of manners. "Thought you were leavin', don't you have a flight to catch? The big ol' world ain't gonna wait for you. Ain't that what you're always tellin' me?"

Meg automatically put down a paper napkin in front of Garrett then placed a cup on top of it. He nodded at Billy, then was suddenly struck dumb at Meg's presence. She wasn't classically beautiful, and many might have called her ordinary but, to Garrett, she was the most wonderful thing he'd ever laid eyes upon. Perfection, for him, was Megan Meyer with her shoulder length brunette hair, green eyes and dainty pink lips that made his heart flutter every time she smiled.

"Cat got your tongue, sexy?" she winked, filling his cup. "Maybe a batch of waffles will get you talking. Or," she smiled, "maybe one of my bagels. Just baked 'em too."

That was all it took, that smile. And the want of a bagel.

He placed all hope on whatever his heart told him to do in the heat of the moment. The only certainty was that it *was* going to happen and it would be today. Traditionally, he considered, on one knee? Among all the customers in here, that'd be pretty attention-seeking and that wasn't his style. Maybe he'd attach it to the check. When she collected it afterwards, she'd see it and realise his intentions. Or he could just take her to one side and ask.

"Honey, if you don't choose soon," Meg went on, "you'll miss your flight. I could choose for you."

"Do that," he finally found his voice. "But make it a bagel, please."

"Just wanted something to eat," Garrett finally answered Billy. "Man needs to eat at a time like this. You lost all your manners, little brother?"

"What?"

"You eat with your hat on? Place is filled with ladies and you eat with your hat on."

Billy removed it quickly. "No point in me even tryin' to be as perfect as you, is there?"

"Your brother's just a slob, Garrett," Meg said setting down a fresh bagel. Just the look of it made his mouth water. "No point in trying to change him now, I guess. You're about the only decent thing to come out of the Cobb household, you and your dear sweet ma, o'course, God rest her soul."

Hearing Meg speak that way of his mother made his heart swell with pride. Knowledge of their father's reputation was common in town; it didn't bother him to hear anybody badmouthing him. It was all truth.

"Ma's sitting on a cloud right now looking down at you, Billy," Garrett said.

"Yeah?"

"Yeah."

"And is she proud of what she sees?"

"Proud as any mama would be who taught her boy manners and sees he don't use 'em."

"Guess with a daddy like ours," Billy defended himself quickly, "kid's gonna learn a few bad habits 'long the way."

"Well, Garrett don't have bad habits, Billy," Meg interrupted. "He's good and proper as any girl could want."

Garrett's heart skipped a beat. That had been a good move. He took a bite of the bagel feeling the ring virtually scald a hole right through to his heart. His heart pounded but life looked good.

"If my big brother is so darned good, Megan Meyer, ask yourself why the hell ain't you still with him?"

And then it all went bad.

"Meg can be with whoever she wants to be with. Ain't nobody's choice but hers."

"I'd better get back to work," she said. "Got dishes out there need washin'."

"You're still leaving today, ain't ya?" The tiniest edge of worry laced Billy voice.

"Flight's leavin' tonight."

"Make sure you're on it."

"You just can't wait for me to be out of the picture, can you?" He looked up to make sure Meg was out of earshot. "Am I that much of a threat to your love-life?"

"Man like me ain't threatened by a man like you."

He looked Billy square in the eye. "Maybe you ought to be."

"No point, not if you're really leaving."

"I'm coming back," he assured him. "Travelling's just for a few months. Just need to see what else is out there. It might not feel like it, y'know, here in Maynard, but out there we're very small fishes in a very large pond." He looked outside, watched the traffic come and go, people walking past the diner going about their business. Maynard was just one small town in a very large state in a huge country. There had to be more to the world than this. "Don't you wanna see what else is out there?"

"Ain't never had the urge. Maynard is plenty 'nuff for me."

"Maybe you should come with me, bro."

"And maybe you should go alone," Billy finished off the last of his waffle and downed the final drops of coffee. "'Sides, if I left, who'd take care of the baby?"

"What baby?"

Meg reappeared with an apologetic smile that made her look older than her twenty-one years.

"I'm going to be a mama."

"And I'm going to be a pa!" The wrong kind of pride covered Billy's face. This was one-upmanship.

"C-congratulations, Meg." He wanted to smile but was unable to produce anything that seemed remotely like pleasure.

Billy had ruined everything. Again.

"I knew you'd understand. I wanted Billy to tell you a month ago, but he just wouldn't."

Garrett stared at him. This was low, even for him.

"I guess my kid brother was waiting for just the right moment."

"Yup. Looks like I found it too. Ain't it time you were leaving?"

"I'll go when I'm ready." He put his hand in his jeans pocket and took out a few dollars placing them next to his cup.

"Oh, Garrett," Meg sighed. "This one's on me. I ain't likely to bake you another bagel in a very long time. Time you get back from your travels, I'll be as big as a dumpling and I sure won't be working in here."

He watched as Meg stroked her flat stomach emphasising her newly announced condition. He'd bet the entire steer in Texas she'd either be working here in six months or working someplace else and he'd never wanted to be wrong so much in his life.

Then a whirlwind of ideas flew through his mind. What if he dropped the whole stupid idea of leaving at all? He could take care of Meg and the baby and to hell with Billy. They could be a family just like they should have been in the first place. Then common sense kicked in. He wasn't part of her life anymore and with Garrett out of the picture, Billy would be forced into responsibility.

He took a deep breath and stood to his feet. Since she wouldn't accept any money for the food, he couldn't offer her the ring on the check and now was most definitely not the time to get down on one knee. Garrett stared at her holding his Stetson between trembling fingers. The ring had gained weight or else the emotional punch he'd received was weighing him down. He hadn't felt this deflated since Meg left him.

"Well, I guess this is it."

"I can't believe I won't see you for six months," Meg said. "It'll seem like a lifetime."

"And the sooner he goes the better," Billy added.

"It'll go quick," he promised. "I've just gotta do it or I'll never do it. I promise I'll be back before you even know I've gone."

Meg kissed his cheek and threw her arms around him. The scent of her perfume filled his nostrils. Holding her like this was going to have to last him a long time. He closed his eyes drinking in all she was. He could feel her warm body against his and more than anything he didn't want the hug to stop.

"Oh my God, I'm gonna miss you so much!" She wiped away an accidental tear giggling away her embarrassment. "I didn't expect to be like this, you must think me lame."

"You take good care of yourself and your baby. I want to hear all about it when I get back."

She pulled away, looked him in the eye and whispered, "You could stay."

"And you could come with me. Please," he begged. "Come with me."

"I've got responsibilities now," she stroked her yet-to-expand tummy again.

He wanted to say, 'marry me' but, "I'll miss you", came out instead.

She released him, wiped her cheek and stood next to Billy as if the position suggested loyalty.

"Goodbye," she said.

"Bye, Meg."

That was the last time he set eyes on her beautiful face. He'd called Billy from every city checking on Meg's progress and to ensure he and Hank were still breathing. A week before his plane touched down, Billy told him he was an uncle. Laura Junior – a tribute to their mother – had been born. Laura senior would have taken great pride in the gesture.

And now, sitting inside his truck outside the diner, Garrett had to get his head into gear. Thinking about the past wasn't useful. He needed a logical, not emotional, approach to

the child who should have been his daughter
not his niece.

He climbed out of his truck as the sun
gained height in the enormous Texas sky.

Chapter Two

If he was wrong and Meg wasn't working in there, he'd gladly eat his words but if he was right and she was…

He pushed open the door to the aroma of freshly brewed coffee and a row of old and new faces. Dirk Henry and his two boys, Chris and Dan – old regulars – sat at one end drinking coffee and eating pie. At the other end were faces he didn't recognise. They looked up; chances were they knew him already by way of the Cobb reputation. The unfamiliar faces went back to their food while Dirk yelled in surprise at Garrett's presence.

"Well, look who just turned up out of the blue!" He stood to shake Garrett's hand, almost breaking every bone in it before he was through. "Been a long time, son. You back for good or just passing through? I hear Billy's a daddy now. Never seemed the type to settle down but I guess we'll see soon enough. How about you, son, isn't it time for you to lay down some roots of your own?"

That was just like Dirk. Why ask one question when you could reel off fifteen in one go?

It was a good welcome. He took off his hat and laid it on the counter. His dirty-blonde hair needed a trim but his blue eyes – his mother's genes – gave away his contentment. He looked healthy and muscular as though he'd spent the last six months working the ranches instead of travelling through Europe.

"It has been a while but it sure feels good to be back. There's something about Maynard that you just can't up and leave and not expect to come home someday."

"She's in your blood, son. Can't give up on Texas, she won't let you," he laughed smacking Garrett's shoulder with the strength of a man half his age. "You get it out of your system?"

"I think so," he nodded.

"Shame Billy wasn't blessed with your mama's genes. That boy needs a reality check if you ask me. Let me buy you a cup of coffee. Sal!" he called behind the counter, "got a customer for you."

"Sal?" Garrett's face fell at the idea of no Meg. "She new?"

"Took over after little Meggie left to have her baby," he explained. "Must've been a week ago by now. Guess that makes you an uncle." He slapped Garrett's chest again and winked at his sons. "Who'd have thought Garrett Cobb would ever be an uncle? Pretty little thing, she is too. We sure miss Meggie in here though." Then he whispered, "She ain't half as good with those bagels."

"Morning, honey." Sal was an older woman who had at least thirty-five years on Meg. Long, wavy copper-coloured hair and a blatant bosom busting from her neckline suggested she'd need good come-backs to go with the attention she would likely attract. But by the look on Dirk's face, he was just as happy at the new sight. "Can I get you some fresh coffee?"

"Thank you."

"You new in town?" she asked.

"I was about to ask you the same."

"I asked first," she smiled. "'Cause I know I've not seen your handsome face before. Man, I would've remembered a sight like you."

Garrett grinned. "No ma'am, Maynard born and bred. I've been away but I'm back now."

"Well, I sure am glad to hear that."

"He's a good boy," Dirk put in. "Known him since the day he was born. Got bitten by the travel bug but he's back for good now, ain't you, son?"

"Yes, sir, I think I am."

"A man needs to see the world before he settles down," she agreed, "sew his seeds and all but it'd be nice to have a good-looking new face around town instead of looking at this old goat all the time."

"Sal, if you want a toy boy to play with, I got two sons sitting right here who'd do you proud. One's fixed up but the other's still free."

Twenty-year-old Dan's shyness forced him to redden at the thought of his dad flirting. Chris Henry, Dirk's married son, grinned but his neat blonde hair made him look eight years old instead of twenty-five.

"I think I'd frighten them away with one kiss," Sal said, then gave Garrett the once over. "But I'll take this one. He's more my type."

"Sorry, ma'am," Garrett joined in the fun, "but I'm already spoken for."

"You are? Oh, that is a disappointment. You're just breakin' my heart today, honey. I hate her already and I ain't even met her."

"You found yourself a girl while you were travellin'?" Dirk asked, plain as day. Like Hank, he never found a reason to beat about the bush.

"Kinda."

"Well, did you bring her back with you? I wanna meet the girl."

"Not exactly."

"Well, you ain't tellin' me much, are you?"

"No, sir, I'm not."

"And that's deliberate, ain't it?"

"Yes, it is." Garrett laughed, drained his cup and stood.

"You off already?"

"Got a lot to do now I'm back."

"I'll bet you do. Better talk to that little brother of yours though. I hear he's been bit by that travellin' bug too now. What is it with you Cobb boys? Your daddy weren't so wayward that he couldn't keep his feet on the ground."

No, Garrett thought, *he was too busy planting his feet by the bar.*

"They off somewhere?"

"Only, what I heard in the bar." Dirk lifted his hands in surrender. "Didn't hear much though and you didn't hear it from me, neither."

Garrett eyed him curiously. Surely Billy wasn't thinking of moving out of the house.

The Cobb ranch was plenty big enough for all of them. If Billy was thinking of moving, why now? Wouldn't it make better sense to wait until the baby was a little older?

"Thanks for the coffee," he said.

"Good to see you back."

"Don't forget to come back soon, honey," Sal waved. "And don't be a stranger."

Ten minutes later Garrett was outside his house, the very house in which his mother gave birth to him. Hank had built it with help from Dirk forty years ago. It was constructed next to the ranch where both Garrett and his brother spent their childhood learning how to rear steer, ride horses and tend the ranch before Hank's business got lost and Garrett turned to construction.

It was a large house yet looked small compared to some of the places he'd visited. He hesitated for a moment before wrapping his knuckles against the wood. Maybe Meg considered it her place now? There was no answer so he pushed the door open. Surprisingly, it was quiet inside, and clean. That was a woman's touch. It smelled nice too, so, no beer spillages left to dry naturally. He was curious, were Billy and Hank even still living here?

"Hello?" he called out in a stage whisper. "Anybody home?"

He headed down the hallway towards the bedrooms, his boots loud on the terracotta tiles. If that didn't wake the dead, nothing would. All the doors were closed and since he didn't know which room Billy and Meg

occupied, he didn't know which one to enter
first. He guessed his old room would still be
unoccupied.

"Hello?" he called again, this time a little
louder.

At the end of the hallway he turned around
and headed back to the den. As he looked
around something stood out. There was
nothing of Meg's here. No pictures, no crafts,
no toys, no baby equipment, nothing. Surely
Meg *was* living here with Billy and Hank?
The only evidence of a woman's presence
seemed to be the lack of dirt.

He turned back again towards his old
bedroom and cautiously pushed open the door,
hoping nobody had taken up residence. The
room was vacant and nothing had changed
from the moment he'd packed his bags to now.
He laid on his bed, put his hat on the
nightstand and closed his eyes for a moment.
No matter where you went in the world,
whichever place you visited, there was
nothing quite like the feeling of your own bed
beneath your body. Garrett breathed in hard
then let it out and, sensing someone watching
him, opened his eyes with a start.

"You're back!" Meg's soft voice came at
him all at once. She stood in the doorway like
a vision in a white lace nightgown; beautiful
and feminine. Standing with one arm on the
door and the other on her post-pregnant
stomach, she smiled. "I can't believe you're
back."

Garrett sat upright unable to speak for a
moment. How he wished she'd grown ugly

during his absence, it would have eased his continued heartache but she was even more beautiful than the last time he'd seen her.

"I didn't know you were due today. I thought I'd have more time." When she threw her arms around him, he took the opportunity to breathe her in. God, she smelled good. "I'd have made the place pretty for you, if I'd known."

He wanted to laugh, the place was fine. "Didn't Billy tell you I was coming back today?"

She rolled her eyes. "Your brother doesn't tell me much of anything, Garrett. Well, other than when he wants feedin'."

He wanted to say a hundred things to her, more than a hundred, a thousand. He wanted to ask her how the pregnancy had been, how labour was, how was the baby. Everything. But only one thing came out.

"How's he been treatin' you?"

She forced a smile nodding eagerly though it was obviously for show.

"And my father?"

She didn't need to say anything regarding Hank either. Her expression said it all. Then she did speak.

"We're doin' just fine. It ain't heavenly or nothin', but I guess a girl like me can't hope for heavenly."

He wanted to apologise. Tell her it was all going to be okay now he was back. He would make it heavenly for her. She deserved heavenly.

He stood. His height was intimidating, but his six-feet-three frame was something she'd missed. Having Garrett stand so close made her forget herself for a moment.

"I'm sorry," he said eagerly. "I didn't ask how the baby is. Is she sleeping? Can I see her?"

"Yes to both."

"Where is she?"

"She sleeps with me in my room." She walked towards the room at the end of the hall. Garrett followed.

"Your room? You don't sleep with Billy?" he asked, then added quickly, "Sorry, it ain't my business. I didn't mean…"

"It's okay," she nodded, opening the door to the smallest bedroom in the house where the boys played as youngsters. She had managed to cram in a single bed and a cradle. The cradle was painted white with tiny pink flowers around the edge and inside that was the tiniest, cutest, pinkest baby girl Garrett ever laid eyes on. Her lips moved as she dreamed.

"Oh my God, she's incredible."

Meg laughed. "I knew you'd say that. You want to hold her?"

"But she's sleeping."

"She's pretty good. You want to?"

"What if I drop her?"

"You won't. She's not as fragile as she looks and I have a feeling you'd be just fine with her." She lifted the baby up holding the covers around her and placed her delicately into Garrett's muscular arms. She looked as if she belonged there. "See, she's quite happy."

"She's amazing. She smells so fresh, so new."

Meg smirked. "Give her half an hour!"

He looked down at the baby's face. Her cute button nose was exactly the same shape as her mother's and so were her lips. He was pleased to notice there wasn't a single thing about Laura Junior that looked anything like Billy.

"She looks just like you. I can't believe she's here. She's so perfect," he grinned in awe.

"She'll be waking up in five minutes for her feed. You want to do the honours?"

"Dare I?"

"You'll enjoy it. She's a good feeder and barely cries."

"I can't believe you produced something this perfect."

She giggled and slapped his arm at the comment. The touch of him was alluring. Just being this close was intoxicating after all this time. "I'm not all bad."

How Garrett had missed that giggle.

"I didn't mean…"

"It's okay, I'll go get her bottle. She didn't take to the breast so I have to feed her with formula."

"Is that okay for her? I mean, why wouldn't she take to it? Is she alright?"

"She's fine. Some babies just don't. She's still getting everything she needs. I'll be right back. She's doing well." Meg walked down the hall, still waddling as if she were heavily pregnant, he noticed. That amused him. She must have gotten used to it. It was kind of cute. She called from the kitchen. "She's already put on half a pound since we left hospital."

At that moment LJ murmured and Garrett's heart skipped a beat.

"Hey, little one. I'm your uncle Garrett. I've been away for a long time so I didn't see you growing inside your mommy's tummy but I'm here now and I'm going to make it all up to you. You want me to give you some breakfast?"

LJ wrinkled up her face and made noises like she was trying to cry. Suddenly she opened her dark blue eyes and looked at him for the briefest of moments. Garrett's heart melted there and then. Before too many noises escaped she took a deep breath, filled her tiny lungs and let out a long loud cry.

"Er, Meg, I think she wants you."

Meg returned with the bottle, grinning.

"Men!" she laughed. "You hear one cry and can't handle it." She took LJ from him and held her close easing the bottle between the baby's lips. Her cries were replaced with sucking.

"Where's Billy?" Garrett asked.

"Asleep I guess."

"Doesn't he help?"

Meg looked away quickly, back to her daughter's face.

"There's nothing I want him to do anyway. We're getting along just fine on our own, ain't we, honey?"

He watched the two together, mother and child. She was perfect at this. He couldn't believe how well she'd taken to motherhood but it suited her. It was just a dire shame it wasn't his child she was feeding.

"On your own? Christ, Meg, Billy helped make her, doesn't he do anything?"

"He spends a lot of time with your father. The two are together a lot these days."

"Billy never said anything. Is Dad okay?"

"Yeah, I mean they go drinkin' together."

"Drinkin'?" he arched a curious eyebrow.

"They're in the bar downtown every night. They've been doing that for a few weeks now. I didn't see Billy leading up to the birth and then…"

"Wait a minute! What do you mean you didn't see him?"

"I didn't move in straight away," she admitted. "After you left things were fine for about a minute. Then Billy and I broke up but I couldn't stay living at my mama's anymore. The place just wasn't big enough and she wasn't happy about the situation. She said I was Billy's responsibility now, not hers, so I called him and said I needed for him to take care of us."

"Meg, I'm so sorry. I can't believe he didn't bring you here straight away."

"I don't think he thought that far ahead. He didn't want much to do with me for a while, he even dated a couple of girls in town but I managed to convince him that he needed to help me. Ever since I've been here though, the two of 'em's been drinking every night. I could put it down to wetting the baby's head but I'm not stupid. That's why he's sleeping in now. Same for your dad, I guess, though he hardly says a word to me anyway."

"And let me guess. Now you're here, you're cooking and cleaning for them both?"

"You got it," she said through thin lips. "I think it's the only reason I'm here. But, hey, I don't mind. I truly don't. It's how I help out. We have a room of our own, LJ's healthy and we're doin' just fine."

"Meg—" He took her chin his between his index finger and thumb.

"Don't say nothin'." She looked into his eyes, aware of the point he was making. "I know how it looks but just don't say it."

Garrett didn't respond. If his face revealed even part of what his heart was feeling it was obvious what he thought.

"So, enough of my gripin', tell me about the world. Was it as good as you wanted it to be?"

"Nothing like this," he said. "There are some weird places out there."

"Did you meet any gorgeous young women?"

"Yeah, a few."

"And?"

"And nothing."

"Well, that's kinda disappointing. I thought you'd meet someone and run off into the sunset. There has to be a million places more interesting than Maynard, Texas. What's France like?"

"French."

"London?"

"English," he laughed.

"I'm not going to get anything out of you, am I?" she smiled. "Well, at least Maynard will be a whole lot more interesting now you're back. Please tell me you're here to stay though, Garrett. I could sure use some sanity in my life right about now."

"I'm back where I belong. God, I've missed you, Meg."

She smiled softly. "I've missed you too. You've no idea just how much. I wanted so many times to call you. I needed to talk so many times."

He understood. He needed to speak to her as well. If they'd ever talked about their break up instead of glossing over it, they might have been back together by now.

"I called Billy a few times. I asked after you but he never said much and he certainly didn't tell me about how he's been treatin' you. What about Chris Henry's wife, Carla? Did you see her much? Their baby must be getting big now. What is he, like a year already?"

"Tommy's two now, he's getting' real big."

"Two?" he said. "How the hell did that happen? I remember buying Chris a beer the night Tommy was born."

"He was born two years ago. You've been away almost a year of that, Garrett. You've missed a lot."

"I certainly did." He stepped closer embracing her unexpectedly. "But I'm back now and things are going to be different."

"We'll get by, Garrett, were gonna do just fine me and LJ."

"Just you and LJ?" he repeated, stepping back. "What about Billy? He *is* her father."

"There's no talking to your brother. If he ever wanted to be a daddy, I've not seen the evidence. You've held her longer than he has."

"I don't believe it." He scowled, raking his fingers through his hair. "I'll talk to him."

"Why?" she shrugged. "There's no point. He's not ready to be a man yet. You can't force him to grow up just 'cause you want him to."

"He was ready to be man the night he took you from me, so let him stand up now and take responsibility for his child." He walked over to the window and peered through the net. The March sunshine warmed the windowpane in front of him. "I'm sorry. I guess I'm still a little bitter."

Meg was silent.

"It was hard enough leaving you at all without finding out a few hours before I left that you were carrying my brother's child. I couldn't think about anything else during the flight. I couldn't think straight for days."

"You shouldn't have been told about the baby like that. I wanted to tell you sooner but Billy just kept saying no. I didn't know what else to do. I'm so sorry I put you through that."

"You know what I'm sorrier about? I hate the fact that I didn't put up a fight to keep you, Meg. I wanted to take you with me. I wanted us to travel, see the world together. I loved you then and I still—"

"God, Garrett, no!" she stopped him, tears in her eyes. "Please don't say it! I can handle the situation I'm in with Billy and I can handle taking care of LJ on my own but please don't tell me you still love me after everything I've put you through. I really don't think I could handle that. Not right now."

LJ finished off the bottle and went back to sleep. Meg put her down and covered her body with the pink cotton sheet. "She'll sleep for a few hours now. Come on, let's go outside."

She put on her dressing gown and followed him to the den.

"Why isn't there more baby equipment here?"

"You've seen what I own. Everything's in the bedroom."

"What about a car seat for the truck? A stroller?"

"I borrowed Carla's seat when I left the hospital, I gave it back. We don't go out much but when we do I walk her in Tommy's old stroller."

"We're miles from the nearest town. Doesn't she have toys?"

"She's barely a week old, she doesn't need toys. All the money I saved after I left the diner I used. I had to live on something. My mom bought a couple of things for us and friends have given us bedding and clothes but other than that, no. When she's a little older, I'll get another job."

"What? My brother's in there sleeping off a hangover and you're thinking of getting a job to support his child?"

"She's my child too."

"But she's half his!" He stood abruptly. "I've heard enough."

"Where are you going?"

"To get his lazy butt out of bed!"

Garrett stormed down the hallway, threw open Billy's bedroom door, yanked the covers off and pushed his body onto the floor. He'd slept in clothes from the night before.

"Get up!"

"What?" Billy's tired eyes were barely open. "What the hell?"

"Get out of bed, you lazy son-of-a-bitch!"

"Garrett? You're back?"

Garrett stood legs apart, arms on hips and temper fuming. "You bet I'm back! What the hell do you think you're doin'?"

"What? What's goin' on?"

"You got a job?"

"No." Billy crawled to his knees and tried to stand up. His hair was stuck in all directions and from the smell of him, he hadn't washed in days.

"You've got no job?"

"No."

"Yet you have a kid to support?"

"I guess."

"You guess?" Garrett walked behind him and kicked his backside until he stood up.

"Get your butt out there. I want you to see somethin'."

"What?"

"Get!"

Billy stood up, rubbing the sleep from his eyes. Frogmarched by his brother, he went into the den. Meg was standing there, her face plastered with confusion.

"You see that?"

"What?"

He took Billy's face in his hands and forced him to look at Meg.

"Meg! You see Meg?"

"Yeah, course I see her. I ain't blind."

"Good. Now what *don't* you see?"

"I ain't playin' games with you," Billy groaned rubbing his head. "I've got a hangover."

"I know and that's exactly why you're gonna get a job. Meg needs things for the baby and you're supposed to be providin' for her, not letting her use hand-me-downs while you're gettin' drunk every night, followin' in your daddy's footsteps."

"A job?"

"Yeah, a job."

"What? Like now?"

"Yeah, right now. Go get showered. I want you back here in ten minutes or I promise you you're gonna feel worse that you do now."

Billy, still half asleep, turned around and walked back to his room.

"The bathroom's that way!" Garrett yelled pointing in the opposite direction.

"You'll wake LJ," Meg scolded.

"I'm sorry." He sighed hard and walked towards her. "I didn't know things were like this. If I'd have known, I promise you I would have been back long ago."

"It's not up to you to take care of us. We're not your problem."

"You're nobody's 'problem', Meg, you're part of our family now. Remember that. And while you're living under the Cobb roof, I don't care what my brother says or does, you and LJ will be cared for."

And with that, Garrett marched to his father's bedroom and pushed open the door with such force the photograph on the wall of his late mother shook.

Garrett Cobb was definitely back.

Chapter Three

Billy was up and dressed within ten minutes. It was better than the consequences, but he still didn't smell good as he dragged himself into the kitchen.

"I'm back barely five minutes and already you've managed to piss me off." Garrett poured coffee into a cup so hastily it flowed over the edges. "Here, drink this. It'll help sober you up."

"I am sober," Billy whined.

"You don't smell it. What's the matter with you anyhow? You've got a pretty girl in there who's taking care of your kid while you go out drinking. Didn't Dad teach you anything while I was away?"

"Yeah," Billy laughed, "he taught me how to drink."

"You think this is funny? You think this is a joke, Billy?"

"It's a little funny," Billy continued. "You have to see the funny side of it. Dad's a drunk," Billy shrugged, "and I'm goin' the same way."

It wasn't exactly the welcome home Garrett imagined. This was a mess. He'd seen Billy hung-over before, but this was a step further into the darkness. He was becoming a carbon copy of their father and Garrett had spent his early twenties retrieving Hank from bars where he'd been kicked out because he couldn't stand or even speak. Garrett took a breath. Once upon a time he was a muscular rancher and now Hank had dissolved into a skin-wrapped skeleton. As much as Billy wearied him, he couldn't let that happen to him too.

"You've got to get yourself back on track, man. And if you can't do it for yourself or Meg, you've got to do it for your kid."

"I can give up any time I want, big brother. I just don't want."

"You'd give up Meg and LJ for the sake of a bottle?"

"When you put it like that."

"Booze has torn this family apart. Didn't you learn anything from the last eight years?"

Billy was just twelve when the barkeeper phoned Garrett that night. Hank was beyond drunk and couldn't stand or speak so Garrett picked him up on the way to getting his mother from her job at the diner. By the time he got Hank inside the truck, Laura had already begun walking. The police report stated a drunk driver had hit her and she was dead on arrival at the hospital. It should have been Hank's funeral that month, not hers. At twenty years old Garrett stepped up to the role of raising his twelve-year-old brother.

"Mama would die all over again if she saw you like this."

"Yeah, well, she ain't here is she?"

"If she was I'd bet you wouldn't be. She'd have thrown you out long ago and been applauded for it too. Dad as well. The two of you are losers, you know what, I don't know why I'm even bothering." He watched Meg walk in pulling a white cardigan across the pink summer dress she wore. Then it dawned

on him why he was bothering; it was for her.
"Okay, get the rest of this coffee inside you
and we're gonna go find you a job."

"You're both going?" Meg asked,
crestfallen.

"Big brother's back in town so everyone
has to jump," Billy whined, "you know how it
is."

"I was hoping you'd stick around here
today. I wanted a little company. I still wanna
hear about all those exciting places you've
been to."

"I'll be back later, Meg, I promise."
Without thinking, Garrett planted a light kiss
on her forehead. She was warm and soft and
smelled amazing. As they parted, they stared
wide-eyed at each other.

"You two wanna be alone?" Billy's cynical
voice sliced through the air like a knife.

"Shut up." Garrett grabbed his jacket and
headed for the door. "I'll be in the truck. Don't
be long."

Billy rolled his eyes and took a leisurely
sip of his coffee. "Didn't take long for him to
get back into it. The man should've stayed
away. Nobody wants him here anyhow."

Meg watched Garrett walk out to his truck.
His muscular thighs caught her attention with
their long strides.

"He lives here, Billy. 'Sides, he's only
doing this to help us or are you too blind to
see that?"

"He's doing this to make himself look
good. So don't you go kidding yourself it's for
anything other reason."

"Why would he do that?"

"'Cause that's what he does. It's all he ever does. It's sickening if you ask me. Garrett Cobb cares only about Garrett Cobb. Period."

"That ain't true at all and you know it."

"Hey, instead of gawping at my brother's ass, don't you have a baby to feed?"

Meg glared. "She's been fed. She's down again. You'd know that if you'd been up an hour ago instead of sleeping off another hangover."

"Clean the damn house then. Just make yourself useful if you insist on staying here." He threw down the cup and headed to the truck.

"If I what? You've got to be kidding me. How dare you, Billy Cobb," she yelled out the door after him. "How dare you!"

Inside the truck, Garrett barked, "What the hell did you just say to her?"

"It ain't none of your business what I said to her."

The brothers drove in silence into town stopping only once for gas. While paying, Garrett asked the owner if help was wanted. The owner peered over Garrett's shoulder, saw Billy Cobb in the passenger seat and declined. Enquiring at the hardware store turned up the same results. The truth of it was Billy wasn't good at anything but messing with everyone's lives. If he could be hired to do that, he'd excel.

Garrett's last port of call was the lumber yard and construction site five miles outside of town. Garrett's old boss Tony Deighton, Carla's father, was a good possibility.

"It's good honest work and you need a job," Garrett told Billy. His tone reverted to the reassuring one he used to give Billy when dealing with homework. "You'll do fine. Give it a month and you'll have money in your pocket plus plenty to give to Meg and LJ."

"I don't want a job."

He handed Billy an application form. "Fill this in. I'll be back."

"Where you goin'? You're just gonna leave me here?"

"I've got to talk to Tony about my old job. Fill that in and come find me after."

Inside the cabin, Garrett stared at plans and blueprints on the walls. Nothing much changed in six months, he thought wryly.

"We've just won the contract to build the new mall," Tony stated proudly. "Took some work, believe me. But you've shown up at the perfect time, Cobb, I could use a man with your skills. I'd be glad to have you back."

"And you'll consider Billy too?"

"I'll talk to the boys in the lumber yard. The boy don't have a great reputation, it's true, and I've got a soft spot for little Meggie but I need your skills so I'm gonna overlook it this once. Plus they owe me a few favours. I guess it's time to collect. Report to me on Monday morning. Bring him too."

Garrett shook Tony's hand. "I appreciate it, I really do."

"Make a note though, if he messes up," he shrugged, "he's gone. It's that simple."

"I understand."

When they got home, Meg was thrilled at the news.

"Maybe I should cook something special for dinner to celebrate. New baby, new job, it's incredible."

Billy nodded. "I'll get some beer in."

"What?" Garrett smirked. "You don't think you and Dad had enough liquor last night?"

"We're celebrating. We can't celebrate without beer."

"No liquor, not with a baby in the house. You'll drink coffee or soda and like it."

"You can't tell me what I can and can't drink. This is my house too."

"Yeah, I can. If you don't like the new rules, Billy, now you've got a job you can save up to buy yourself a place of your own."

Billy sulked. "This is ridiculous!"

"It makes sense," Meg agreed, mixing the baby's formula. "I'm not that thrilled with the idea of liquor in the house anyway. It's not good for LJ to grow up in that environment. And maybe a place of our own would be good for us."

Garrett swallowed hard. He'd forgotten for a brief moment wherever Billy went, Meg would likely follow.

"What the hell has it got to do with you anyhow, Meg? This ain't your house."

"Billy!" Garrett slapped him upside the head. "Don't speak to her like that. Have some respect. She's just given birth to your child."

"I'm getting a little tired of hearing how Meg's done this and Meg's doing that. I got a job didn't I?"

"Your brother got you that job," she was too smug for Billy's taste.

"Well, he's just a regular Superman, ain't he? You know if you two are so into each other, why the hell don't you get back together?"

"Watch your mouth!" Garrett hissed. "You know if you can't keep a civil tongue in your head, you can stay in your room."

"You get back and all of a sudden you're my father?"

"No," Garrett said coolly, "I've been fillin' that role since you were a snot-nosed, twelve-year-old. I raised you from the moment Dad forgot he had a family."

"So, you're gonna ground me?"

"If that's what it takes to get you on the straight and narrow, yeah."

"I'm not a kid anymore, bro, when are you gonna stop treating me like one?"

"When you grow the hell up."

Billy threw down his cup and stormed out. It landed on the table with a loud crack and broke clean in half. Remains of coffee spilled between the halves and Meg reached to clear it up.

"I'm sorry you two can't seem to get along," she said softly. "I didn't think it would be like this when you got back. I had the stupid notion we were all going to get along. I don't know why I thought that. You never did before."

"I'm sorry. I can't seem to stop biting every time he opens his mouth. I thought fatherhood would have changed him for the better, calmed him down maybe."

She took the broken pieces and threw them in the trash. One shard sliced her hand at the base of her index finger but she didn't notice. It was Garrett who saw the blood. Instantly, he took her hand and held it over the sink.

"I didn't even feel it happen."

"Good thing I was here then." He held it underneath the cool running water until the bleeding stopped.

"This is getting to be a habit," she looked up at him. Garrett's face was so close she could see his chin beginning to show signs of a shadow. He smelled earthy and masculine. It was a sensual change from Billy's liquor-coated stench. She stared into his blue eyes. Tiny flecks of copper reflected the sunshine coming through the kitchen window. If he tried to kiss her now, she wouldn't stop him.

"What is?"

"Your brother causes all these problems and you come along like a knight in shining armour and fix everything."

"I don't think I'm that saintly. I just see an issue and do my best to fix it. A knight in shining armour, huh? Is that how you think it looks?"

"Isn't that how you want it to look?" she asked, recalling Billy's earlier comment.

"What do you mean?"

"Nothing, I'm just saying."

"Meg, I just want the best for you and LJ. That's all I ever wanted."

"Why? We're not your responsibility, Garrett." Her hand grew cold under the water and she pulled it back, wrapping it in the towel. "I stopped being your responsibility the night I slept with your brother."

"Don't say that."

"It's the truth. If I hadn't made that choice that night, you and I would still be together."

And married.

Garrett turned away. He couldn't bear to hear her words.

"You know what I was going to do the day I left? I was going to propose to you."

"What?" she gasped. She'd wanted to hear that proposal so many times during her pregnancy but he wasn't there to whisk her away any more. One bad decision had changed her entire life. "What if I'd have said yes? You were getting on a plane that night."

"I had another ticket. I had it in the truck waiting just in case you did. It was pretty lonely on that flight, believe me," he said softly. "I had it all planned. You'd say yes and we'd fly off into the sunset just like we were supposed to."

Her face turned red as tears blurred her vision. He pulled her close and kissed the top of her head.

"I had this stupid romantic plan that we were going to run away together. But then," he added, "Billy said you were pregnant."

The soft caresses of his shirt against her cheek were alluring and the smell of his hard chest beneath it was home to her. He pulled her away gently grasping her cheeks in his hands. She lifted up her head for him to claim her lips but just as he touched them LJ began crying. Garrett, pulled away, his heart pounding.

Meg stared, disappointed. "She wants her supper."

He watched her walk away knowing full well where it would have ended up if LJ hadn't cried when she did.

And he so badly wanted it to end up like that.

Chapter Four

Hearing a baby's cry was a strange but comforting sound in the house. Garrett made his way through the hall and stood just outside Meg's door. It was ajar by three inches or so and he watched her feeding LJ through the gap.

"You can come in if you like," Meg called over LJ's inconsistent cries. "I won't bite, I promise."

He pushed the door open a little more but didn't progress inside, instead he leaned against the doorway with crossed arms over his chest.

"How's your hand?"

"It's okay."

"Shall I order take-out?" he asked. "I don't think anyone's up to cooking tonight and the cupboards are pretty bare."

"That's my fault," she nodded. "I planned to get some groceries in today but you kind of surprised me coming back this morning. If I'd have known you were back today I'd have gotten something in."

"Meg, it's not up to you to stock the cupboards. We all eat so we all help out." Then he laughed.

"What's so funny?"

"They expect you to run around after them all the time don't they?"

She smiled. "I guess that makes me a little lame, huh?"

"Put-upon I'd say. They've been taking advantage of your good nature."

"Well, in their defence I have been out of hospital for over a week now, I should help out where I can."

"In *their* defence?" he almost stumbled over the words. "Don't go defending them. They don't deserve it. Tomorrow I'll get some groceries in and if the two of you are feeling up to it, I'm going to take you with me. I guess you could use some extra baby supplies, right?"

Meg nodded. "We always need diapers. But you really don't have to do that, Garrett. Billy's got a job now, things will get better. We'll do fine."

"I'm sure you will but you should know by now, Meg, once I have something in my head there's no talking me out of it. So, what do you want to eat? Chinese? Italian?"

"Pizza," she said. "I'd love pizza with everything on it."

"Why don't you feed her in the den? It'd be nice to see her outside of here for a change."

She lifted the baby and held her over her shoulder with a cloth between her and LJ's rosebud mouth. Garrett followed her, ordered the pizza and sat opposite.

"You know I wanted to say before that I was really touched that you called her LJ. I know Mom would have been thrilled."

"I asked Billy what names he liked but he didn't give me much input. Actually he didn't give me any input."

"Go figure."

"I'd chosen two names, one for a boy and one for a girl."

"Out of curiosity, what was the boy's name?"

"It doesn't matter now."

"I'd still like to know."

"Garrett," she said in a small voice, gauging his reaction. "I was going to name my little boy Garrett."

He was shocked, if slightly touched. "Why?"

She glanced at him with a split-second of that devotion in her eyes she had when they were together.

"Why not?" As if to deflect the moment she added quickly, "But as you might imagine, it didn't go down very well so I'm pretty lucky she was a girl." She looked down at the baby in her arms and smiled. "And I called you Laura Marie Cobb, didn't I? She suited it from the get-go. She was strong, beautiful and wise so Laura fitted perfectly."

Pride drifted over Garrett's face. It made his heart swell to know she thought that much of his mother's memory and of him. Even after everything that had happened.

"Marie, after your mom?"

"Yeah. She was pretty surprised considering she practically threw me out."

Garrett laughed. "Did Garrett Junior have had a middle name?"

"William," she said sourly, before rolling her eyes. "I had to keep everyone happy. The fact that Garrett went before William was another bone of contention."

"And the general fact 'Garrett' was there at all, I'm guessing?"

"It was a silly time. There was all kinds of name-calling flying around. Billy hated me, I hated him and a few months later we're living together trying to at least like each other. Who'd have thought a year ago that I'd be sitting here with this little bundle in my arms?"

"I'm sorry you went through all of that. If I'd have known, I would have been here, you know that don't you. Billy wouldn't have gotten away with treatin' you like he has."

Dinner arrived and he shared it out leaving a slice each for Billy and Hank in the box. Whether or not Billy left his room to join them was his choice but Garrett was certainly happier spending time alone with Meg.

"Shouldn't you call Billy?" she asked.

"Billy!" he yelled then smirked at his instant decision. LJ jumped in Meg's arms and started to cry again. "Oops, sorry! I guess I'm going to have to remember there are some pretty sensitive ears living here now."

Meg hushed the baby and took a bite of pizza, juggling the two. She'd not tasted pizza since she cooked it herself at the diner but it was exquisite all the same.

"Why don't you let me hold her while you eat?" he offered. "I think I can win her over."

She watched as he held LJ up as though she were standing up on his thighs. LJ's tiny face screwed up as she howled at him.

"I think she likes me," he laughed. She seemed so small in his manly hands.

Eventually he held her against his shoulder, feeling her new skin against his own rough chin. "She's precious, isn't she?"

"She certainly is. You might want to hold a towel over your shoulder in case she—" She didn't get any further before LJ spat up his shirt. "Sorry."

"That was fun." He grabbed the cloth and wiped it away. "What does she do for an encore?"

"You don't want to know but it smells a lot worse."

"Me and you are going to have to get a little more acquainted if you're gonna do that again." Her wide-open eyes looked straight at him. "But I have the feeling you and me are already good friends. I'm going to have a hard time keeping the boys away from you."

Meg listened to him. It was as if he considered her his own child. How she wanted that to be true. It was a pity, she thought looking at him. He would make a brilliant father; he was definitely husband material.

"I'll go see if Billy wants his pizza in his room."

"Let him come out here if he wants feedin'." He held LJ above his head and blew raspberries at her puffing out his cheeks.

"I'd rather anyway. I'll be right back."

She put a slice on a plate and walked down the hallway. When she got to Billy's door, Garrett heard her knock. In his opinion, she was way too good to the boy. Ten seconds later she stood in the den staring at Garrett with the plate still in her hands.

"You're not going to believe this, Garrett.
He's gone."

Chapter Five

Garrett handed LJ back and ran to Billy's
room. He needed to see for himself. The bed
was messed up and above the closet the case
was missing. The curtain flapped in the
evening breeze and through the window he
saw the truck was missing.

"I don't believe this. I'll kill him."

Meg came in with LJ over her shoulder.

"Maybe he went out for a drink."

"Through the window?"

"He obviously didn't want to walk past us
in the den to get out. He could've heard us in
the kitchen earlier."

Dirk Henry's words filled his mind, maybe
Billy saw this as his chance to leave Maynard.
Garrett naively presumed it would be with
Meg and LJ.

"Meg, he ain't coming back."

"You don't know that."

"His case is gone and his truck is gone."

"He wouldn't do that. He got a job today,
there's a future now."

"He had a future as soon as he got you
pregnant. The boy's gone. He's left."

"No, he's trouble, sure, but he wouldn't
just abandon us." She sounded scared, alone.

He wanted to hold her, feel her soft skin
against his chest and protect them both from
Billy's foolishness. But he knew it wouldn't
end there. He put one hand on her shoulder
and the other on LJ's silken head.

"I wish I could tell you you're right but
Dirk Henry said Billy's been talking. He said

he wanted to leave Maynard. I thought he meant with you and LJ. I didn't know he'd be so stupid as to up and leave by himself."

"He hasn't said a word." She held LJ closer. "He can't leave us. What am I going to do?"

"You're goin' to be fine, both of you. You've got me and I ain't goin' any place."

"Maybe he's with Hank," she said hopefully. "They're probably drinkin' together at the bar." She never thought she'd be so happy to imagine such a thing.

"I'll go check. You stay here in case he does come back." He kissed her forehead briefly and gave her a reassuring smile.

He was raging. He'd been back a day and still hadn't seen his dad and already he'd broken up a family. He climbed into his truck, leaving the sound of screeching wheels and a plume of dust behind.

It was filled with people inside Langley's. Hot bodies yelled at each other hoping to be heard over the rock and roll on the juke box. He eased his way through dancers, drinkers and others who watched him walk with purpose. Then he spotted Chris and Dirk at the bar. Another family, he noticed, brought together through the medium of liquor. The difference was Dirk knew how to be a father.

"You seen Billy?"

Chris shook his head, perhaps surprised at the abruptness of the question.

"You lost him, son?" Dirk put in.

"I hope not." He smiled, adding a lightness to the situation. "Do you know where else he might hang out?"

"Try Fraser's downtown," Chris offered. "He goes there sometimes. Everything alright?"

"I just need to talk to him."

"Big brother's kicking ass, huh?" Dirk laughed. "Good thing too in my opinion. Your daddy was in here earlier. He ain't looking good, boy. Maybe they're together."

"What time did Dad leave?"

"About a half hour ago and he wasn't in any rush, if you know what I mean."

Garrett knew exactly what he meant. He made his way to Fraser's. If Billy was there, he might have a chance of talking him out of leaving Maynard

Leave it alone and it will soon go away. Billy's teenage words about homework suddenly flew through Garrett's mind. Maybe because the situation hadn't gone away, Billy had instead.

Garrett blamed Hank. He should never have had to raise his own brother. Hank should have taught him how to stand up and fight for what he wanted, not run away from conflict.

In the distance the lights from Fraser's bar shone out like a beacon. If Billy was inside, he'd take him home straight away so the three of them could sit down and talk this thing through like grown adults. The constant bickering and fighting wasn't doing any of them any good.

Garrett pulled into the lot and ran inside. The green and red stained glass panels above the bar shone like church windows. It had been some time since Garrett had graced this place but the last time he did was with Meg. In a moment of nostalgia, he noticed the booth in the corner they shared for three hours, laughing, drinking and joking. It was one of the best nights of his life. Another couple occupied it now.

Scanning the room, he saw one familiar face. It took him a moment to recall where he had seen her before. She had seen him first and abruptly approached him.

"Hey there, Cowboy." A husky voice came out of Sal's grinning face. She stared at all of him from his boots, up to his jeans and then the black T-shirt he wore under his unfastened plaid shirt. "Garrett Cobb, did I get that right?"

"Yes, ma'am, you did."

"Ma'am? Wow that just put a downer on my night. But, I've gotta say it's damn good to see you again. Want to buy me a drink?" She stroked his cheek and purred.

Respectfully, he lowered her hand. "Another time? I'm looking for my brother. Have you seen him?"

She nodded. "He's over there with your daddy."

Billy looked haggard and angry while Hank looked plain ill. His six-feet-one frame seemed too tall for his bony body. He looked like a living skeleton. Garrett wondered how long it had been since he'd washed; both men were an embarrassment to the Cobb name.

"Billy!" he called over the noise.

Billy looked up and his face fell instantly. "What the hell are you doin' here?"

"Why the hell did you leave?"

"I wanted a drink. Is that going to be a problem?"

He looked at his father; he was barely recognisable. "Dad."

"Son." Hank's face barely moved. "I heard you'd come back."

"I can't lie. It would've been nice to see you at home when I arrived."

Hank dismissed the idea with a wave of a shaky, bony hand.

"I didn't know when you were coming back. I can't stay in all day."

"I've not seen you for six months, Dad. I've not even heard your voice. I've missed you."

"Well, I'm here now so you can see all you want to see."

Garrett swallowed back his disappointment of not being welcomed. He didn't dare ask if he'd missed him. How he longed to be embraced like his mother used to when he got home from school. That was love; that was how a parent was meant to be.

"How are you, Dad?"

He shook his head and upturned his mouth. "'Bout ready to meet my maker, I reckon."

Garrett closed his eyes in sadness, trying to breathe slowly and not absorb all the negativity Hank exuded.

"Dad, don't. You've got years yet. Heck, lay off that stuff and maybe even longer."

"And there it is," Billy put in. "Kick-ass Cobb, right here, ladies and gentlemen. Whoa!" He turned to another patron with his hand flat out awaiting a twenty-dollar bill, which was reluctantly slapped into his palm.

"You gambling, bro?"

"Only ones I know I can't lose," he smirked. "I bet this fine man that if my brother showed up, you'd give us a hard time about drinking within five minutes of you being here. I won my bet fair and square."

Garrett was silenced. Billy and Hank simply saw him as the party-pooper, not the brother who raised and nurtured Billy or the son who cooked and cleaned for his father as well as holding down a job to keep them fed and housed. He didn't want thanks, he just wanted a little respect.

"Another, Dad?" Billy leaned over the bar with the twenty. "Bet you're proud of me for the initiative alone. Basically, I won us free drinks. Another for me and my daddy, please, Todd. I'd offer to buy you a drink, dear brother, but you'd probably throw it out before it hit your saintly lips."

"I ain't no saint, Billy, I drink. I just can't do it without thinking about Mama."

Todd filled two beakers with liquor and placed them in front of each of them. Garrett pushed away Hank's before he could drain it in one go.

"What's goin' on?" Hank slurred.

"You've had enough."

"I've had enough, boy, when I say I've had enough." He snatched the glass back.

"See, Dad?" Billy cut in. "Didn't I tell ya?"

"No son of mine is gonna tell me when I can get a drink." He stood, staggered and downed the shot.

"Yeah," Billy added. "Why don't you just leave us and go back travellin'. You ain't welcome here no more."

Garrett was shocked into silence.

"I think Garrett's right, Hank," Todd agreed. "You've had enough. I won't sell you any more tonight."

"Then I'll go to another bar and give them my money."

Billy looked ready to leave with his father.

"Wait," Garrett barked.

"Is this going to be yet another lecture?"

"No, look, I'm sorry I keep kicking your ass but I'm trying to help a lot of people here. I just got off the plane yesterday, Billy, I'm wiped out. I just want to ask you why you left. We'd bought pizza but you'd gone."

"So, I wanted a drink," he shrugged casually. "I already told you. We were goin' to celebrate and since you won't allow liquor in the house now, I got no choice but to go out and get it, do I?"

"You wanted a drink that bad?"

"You judgin' me again?"

This could easily go the same way as all the other conversations had gone but Garrett didn't want to fight.

"No, of course not. I'm tryin' to help you."

"I don't need no help. You come back home, you take my girl and you order me around."

"Is that what you think? Meg and me, we were just talking, just catchin' up. I haven't seen her for six months, man. A lot has happened. She had a baby for Christ's sake."

"I know. And it's *my* kid, not yours."

"Right," Garrett agreed. "So explain to me why you've not been takin' care of them?"

"I don't answer to you."

"No, you answer to Meg. She needs your support."

"Support? We ain't together like that," he announced. "Not like man and wife. Not like it's any of your business anyway."

"You gonna?"

"What?"

"You gonna marry her?"

Billy laughed as if the notion to marry were the stupidest thing he'd ever heard. "Hell, no!"

Garrett tried with all his might not to let every single word that escaped Billy's lips frustrate him. But it was almost impossible. The crowd stopped their own conversations just to listen to theirs. Pretty soon they had an audience.

"You're not goin' to marry her?"

"No plans to."

"What exactly are your plans?"

Billy shrugged. "Ain't given it any thought."

"No kiddin'! Well, you got a job now. Maybe you could take this weekend to think about your plans and talk to Meg about them. Everything you do now concerns her and that little baby girl."

"You're talkin' to the wrong guy, big brother, 'cause I just ain't interested. And I ain't going to the job neither."

"Well, you'd better get interested, Billy, and real quick. There's a woman back there who needs you to be a man for her and a daddy for her kid. Hell, you were a man when you stole her from me so why in God's name can't you be a man now?"

"I don't love her, that's why, hell I don't even like her much."

"Then why the hell did you take her from me?"

The crowd wanted to know the answer almost as much as Garrett.

"Because I could," he said slowly, grinning and lapping up the hate and resentment his brother oozed. "You're pissed, bro, 'cause you're still in love with her and you don't have her and I do but I couldn't give a damn about either of them. I've got what you want and you hate that."

"You're damn right I'm pissed off."

"She was an easy lay too."

Unable to stop himself – or want to – Garrett launched his fist straight into Billy's jaw. His knuckles hurt but it was well worth the pain. Billy fell into the bar stools then onwards to the ground. The crowd went wild.

"Get up and fight like a man, you son-of-a-bitch!"

"You broke my jaw!"

"No I didn't. But give me another shot and I'll do it right!"

Garrett couldn't wait another second and grabbed Billy's shirt by the neck pulling him up to meet his fist. Blood fell from his nose and between his teeth. As Garrett readied his fist for another shot, Todd pulled him off.

"He's down already!" Todd yelled. "That's enough!"

Garrett stood breathlessly, watching over his brother's battered body. He grabbed him to his feet, leaned into his face and looked right into his eyes.

"Go home. *Now!*"

"I'm leaving."

"Good."

"No, I mean I'm leaving Maynard and I ain't comin' back."

Before Garrett could respond, Hank fell off his bar stool and landed on the floor next to Billy. His body was as limp as a ragdoll with a face of deathly grey.

Billy's eyes sprang wide open in shock. "He ain't breathin'."

Chapter Six

"Call an ambulance!" Sal shouted.

Todd picked up the phone while Hank's lifeless body lay on the bar's dark red carpet.

"Is he dead?" Billy whimpered. "Is my daddy dead?"

"Yes," Sal said.

"No, he can't be."

"Well, he ain't breathin'," Garrett said.

The crowd encircled the family, enveloping them in darkness. If the bar was to be Hank's final resting place, he'd have found solace in that.

"Give these men some space," Sal yelled over the noise. "Someone turn off that music, give these men some privacy. Go about your business."

"He drank himself to death," Garrett said finally. "That's all there is to it. It's over."

She felt Hank's neck for a pulse too then looked up at each of the boys in turn. "Wait, I can feel something. No, I don't think he's gone."

"I have my truck outside. It'd be quicker than waiting for the paramedics."

Hank was so frail, Garrett lifted him without any assistance and carried him as though he were an overgrown baby. He ran through the bar, Sal and Billy behind him, and placed his father on the back seat. Billy sat next to him while Sal took the passenger seat next to Garrett.

"This is unbelievable. I'm so sorry."

"Wherever there's a Cobb," Garrett told her, "there's always a problem." He scraped his hair back, feeling sweat running down his back and needing a shower so bad. In the rear-view mirror, Billy was crying. His dark brown hair and sad brown eyes looked exactly as they did when he was a child. The bloody evidence from their fight had dried in streaks down his face. "Hold on, Dad."

He drove like a maniac trying to get to the hospital before it was too late. Once there the staff took over.

"What happened?" the nurse asked.

"He stopped breathin'," Garrett explained.

"What's his name?" the nurse called, as they all ran down the corridor towards the emergency room.

"Hank Cobb."

"His age?"

"Seventy-eight."

"Do you know what happened to him?"

Garrett took off his Stetson and nodded. "Yes, ma'am, he's an alcoholic."

"Are you're his next of kin?" she asked.

"I'm Garrett Cobb. I'm his son and this is my brother, Billy."

She looked at Sal. "Mrs Cobb?"

"No," she confirmed, "just a family friend."

The three of them stood breathless, watching Hank fighting for his life while the hospital staff wheeled him on.

Billy started crying. "Alcoholic?"

"I didn't lie."

"This is all your fault!" he spat out the words like a viper. "If you hadn't come into the bar tonight shouting out your orders, he'd have been fine."

"He was an alcoholic for years. This had nothing to do with me."

"*Was*? Don't you dare speak about him like he's already dead. He was breathin' back there. I saw him breathin'."

Garrett put his hands firmly on his shoulders, forcing him to stay put. "I think you should prepare yourself. Dad ain't leavin' here alive."

"It's true," Sal said, offering her support. "You've got to be strong now. I've seen this a hundred times, honey. Alcoholism is a disease and your daddy's been sick for a long time."

Billy turned red with rage and slapped Sal across her face.

"How dare you, you don't even know him."

Garrett saw red, picked him up from the seat and shook him. "That's enough!" He turned to Sal. "I'm sorry, he's been a little out of control since," he shrugged, "birth."

"The kid's traumatised." She touched her cheek, feeling the sting. "I'm so sorry about your father."

"He did it to himself. The man should've died eight years ago."

"Why eight?"

"Long story."

"Well, we might be here a long time and I'm known in some parts for my sympathetic ear."

"Now ain't the right time." He got Billy to sit back down. He looked every bit as though he'd been in a bar brawl. "We'd better get you cleaned up and get some coffee inside you or we'll be thrown out of here."

"You wait here in case they have some news," Sal said. "I'll see what I can find to clean him up."

Both men took a seat in the waiting room. Garrett buried his face in his hands while his brother stared into space. He was tired and hungry. He'd never quite gotten around to eating the pizza he brought earlier but right now he could down the entire thing without chewing. He suddenly realised Meg would think he was still out looking for Billy. She wouldn't have a clue he was in the hospital waiting on news of their dying father. He held his hat in his hands turning it around by the rim. He'd have to find a payphone and call her, tell her what had happened.

"I'll be back in a minute. Stay here, don't move."

He took out some change from his pocket and fed them into the payphone. Meg answered straight away.

"Did you find him, is he alright?" she asked urgently. In the background, LJ was crying.

"I'm at Mercy Hospital."

"Oh dear God! What happened to him? How bad is it?"

"No, you don't understand, it's my dad. He collapsed. He stopped breathin'." Suddenly he seemed to lose all composure and choked up at the thought of Hank's imminent death. He'd give anything to have Meg's arms hold and comfort him. "Meg, I don't think he's gonna make it."

"Garrett! Oh my God, I'm so sorry. What can I do?"

He coughed away his upset, angry he'd allowed himself to show his vulnerabilities. Hank was a lousy father and a lousier husband to Laura. Garrett shouldn't be feeling sad over this, he should be feeling relief. Blood was absolutely thicker than water.

"How's Billy taking it?"

"Not good."

"I'll ask Carla to bring me."

"No, you can't be here too. You need to stay there and take care of the baby."

"She's fine."

"She's cryin'."

"Missing her daddy, maybe?"

For a moment, he wondered exactly which Cobb brother she meant.

"I've tried putting her down but it's like she knows something's wrong."

"I'll call as soon as I know something."

"I hope so and, Garrett?"

"Yeah."

"Take care of your brother, won't you? He's all LJ and I have."

Her words sliced through his heart. He wanted to yell out as loud as his lungs would allow that he was ready and willing to replace Billy but something in her voice told him it wasn't supposed to be that way. His chance of a future with Meg was over the night she'd

gone with his brother, maybe he'd just better
get used to that after all. Questioning his own
motives left him with a bad taste in his mouth.
If she saw Billy's face right now, she'd
definitely question Garrett's caring abilities.

"Sure."

Sal returned with two cups of coffee and a
moist paper towel.

"It was all I could find." She set about
gently removing the bloodstains.

"I'm sorry I hit you," he said in a tiny
voice.

Garrett extended an olive branch by
placing a compassionate hand on Billy's
shoulder.

"Hang in there, kid."

Chapter Seven

It was a further thirty minutes before a doctor appeared. A middle-aged, scrawny man, who looked as if he should exchange a nightshift for a good meal and a vacation, took off his wire-rimmed glasses to deliver the news.

The three stood as he approached.

"I'm so sorry." He didn't need to elaborate for them to know the outcome; his expression was more than enough. "His liver couldn't take any more."

"Liver failure. Of course. Thank you." Realising the Cobb boys were unable to speak through shock, Sal asked, "Did he regain consciousness at all?"

He nodded. "Who's Garrett?"

Garrett looked up, unable to speak for fear of losing it again, simply nodded. "Your father managed to say one thing. He said to tell Garrett he was sorry. I got the impression you'd understand why."

A large lump grew in Garrett's throat as he covered his mouth and turned away. He leaned against the wall next to the payphone, knee bent, sole flat on the wall. So this was what it was like to be an orphan, even at twenty-nine. It hurt just the same as when his mother died. He always thought it would be a relief when Hank passed away, but it wasn't. He wasn't prepared for the gaping hole Hank left. The man was an unworthy, unreliable and undeserving son-of-a-bitch but, it seemed, blood was blood and nothing could ever change that.

Sal leaned in close and whispered, "Hey buddy, you got home before he went. You got to see him and speak to him. That's gonna help in the coming days."

The last twenty-four hours had been hell on earth on so many levels.

Sal consoled Billy, wrapping her arm around his shoulders and she lowered him to the chair.

The sound of footsteps approaching quickly stirred Garrett. It was Meg. He wiped his face, unaware he'd been crying or for how long, and stood forward to receive her but instead of running to him she offered only the briefest of smiles and comforted Billy. Garrett watched them in their own private grief-stricken world and, inside, he wanted to scream out his anger and resentment. He inhaled sharply, letting it out slowly, unable to remove his eyes from the pair.

"How are you holdin' up, Cowboy?" Sal asked.

"I'm doin' good," he lied, sniffing back tears.

"Shame you ain't good at lying as you are looking good."

"I ain't lyin'. I'm fine. There's nothin' more we can do here. I need to take them home."

"And what about Garrett? What does he need?"

He looked down at her, staring deep into her hazel eyes. At some point during the evening, her hair had been pulled back into a ponytail. She looked as wiped out as them all.

"Maybe I don't need anythin'."

"You know, I've been pondering something. I reckon you're a fixer," she said. "Yeah, that's it. You're a rescuer."

"Excuse me?"

"People take on natural roles in their lives. I think you're one of those people who fixes things for other people and rescues them from their problems."

That'd be him. A rescuer. He'd rescued more people than he could count. If it wasn't his mother, it was his father. Now it was Billy and Meg. But Sal was right, what about Garrett? Who was going to fix his problems?

"I'm a listener," Sal nodded. "That's my thing. I'm pretty good at it too. I heard what you said in the bar. I know what happened between you and your brother but to be honest it wouldn't have taken a genius to work it out."

"None of that matters any more."

"No, you're probably right," she agreed, pursing her lips and staring, like Garrett, at the couple embracing on the chairs. "Don't make it any easier though, does it? You know what you are?"

He had an idea: an idiot probably, a jerk definitely.

"What?"

"One of *the* nicest, most honourable people I've ever met in my life," she said. 'Course it don't hurt you're sexy as hell. But you know what happens to nice people, don't you? They get kicked in the ass."

"I guess they do."

"But in my experience," she went on, "as much as it hurts like hell to get kicked in the ass so much, I still find it's best to be nice. Life kinda sucks that way, don't it?"

Chapter Eight

Carla had been watching LJ in the car. As they piled out of the hospital, Carla took Billy and Meg back leaving Garrett to take Sal home.

It seemed a long slow drive even though Sal lived nearest of all of them to the hospital. Garrett pulled up outside her home, turned off the engine and placed his hands on the wheel. The night had come about without him even realising it. It was starry up there and the moon shone brightly. Was Hank up there now alongside Laura? He sighed re-absorbing the previous hours, trying like hell not to cry again.

"You should come in for a minute," Sal broke the silence. "I'll make you some coffee. You sure look like you need some."

"I feel like I just got trampled on by a raging stampede."

"And that's kind of how you look too, sugar."

"I should thank you."

"For what?"

"I just met you this morning and tonight you helped me keep my dad alive just long enough. I don't know what I would have done without you. Thank you, Sal."

"Come on in and I'll make you that coffee."

"I really should get back. Check they're okay."

"And maybe you should go back to the hospital to see if anybody else needs help." She looked down at her watch. "Hell, there's an hour 'til midnight, maybe they'll give you a white coat and mask so you can assist in the OR?"

"I get it."

"Good," she grinned. "Now get your fine butt out of the truck and into my kitchen. If it takes me all night to get some coffee into you, I'll do it and by golly don't you think for one minute I won't."

"Yes, ma'am."

She lived alone, that much was obvious. He couldn't imagine a man living with her anyway; she was slightly frightening in a compassionate kind of way.

She made coffee while he sat down. A narrow shelf above the banquette and table displayed three photos in frames. The first was of an elderly couple, the second a possible partner and the third was a new-born.

"Cute little thing, ain't he?" She put a mug down in front of him and sat opposite.

Garrett picked up the frame. "Who is he?"

"My son's kid. That photo was taken last year. He'll be getting big now, I reckon. They called him Joshua."

"You don't see him much?"

"They live up north, Nebraska. I see 'em a couple of times a year. They have a life, so do I."

He pointed to the middle one. "Husband?"

"No, this guy wasn't the marrying kind but he was one of the nicest people I ever knew. He was a good friend of mine. I trained to be a counsellor the same time he did. Frank was an amazing guy."

"Was?"

"Yeah," she nodded sadly. "He was killed."

"Killed? How?"

"We worked together as telephone counsellors; remember I said I was a good listener? We used to get the same people call a lot. Frank had this guy call over and over, a junkie. They worked through some horrific issues together and then one night he found out where we were and waited for Frank. It was over pretty quick."

"That's horrible, I'm so sorry."

"Nobody ever said life was goin' to be a bed of roses, did they? But I got to meet Frank and he helped a lot of people over the time he was there. 'Sides Frank's in a better place now, same as your daddy. And the best part is they ain't hurtin' no more."

He tried to absorb the horror of her story while putting aside his own horrific night's events.

"Like you, honey, I was born in Texas. I lived in Houston for a while, then Denver, but I got itchy feet again and literally put a pin in the map," she said. He looked at her ring finger but there was no evidence of anything. "No, never have been, neither. My son was a gift from one of those go-nowhere relationships. The guy took off soon as he found out. Nine months later Kevin was born. He's a good boy. Never wanted for nothin', I gave him as good an upbringin' as I could and that's all anyone can ask."

"You're an amazing woman, Sal."

"Hell, yes I am," she laughed. "Tell me
about yourself, Cowboy. I've known you for
almost an entire day and still I don't know
your life story yet. I'm usually better than that.
You just got back from travellin', huh?"

He nodded. "I needed to get it out of my
system. I've lived here my whole life and I
wanted to see what else was out there ever
since my mom died."

"Eight years ago? And let me guess, your
daddy wasn't much good at fatherin' so you
took on the role instead?" Sal grinned. "I
listen. I watch. I put it all together."

"I had no choice but to step up. Billy was
still a child, he needed rearing right. He
needed help at school, he didn't make friends
easy. Dad propped up a bar more than he
worked. It was tough for a long time. I
stopped working the ranch – it was drying up
anyway, and I got a job in construction. It paid
a lot more and it was better hours. There were
bills to pay and I had to feed us since Dad
kinda just fell off the planet."

"It's a lot for a kid to take on."

"It was a steep learning curve. I learned a
lot about life and how to take care of a
household and a family. I did what I watched
Mama do. She always talked to me when she
cooked or got groceries. Looking back it was
kinda cool that she taught me because after the
funeral, I had no choice but to take care of
them. The way I see it, we got dealt a tough
hand and I was the only one available to step
up. I mean, sure it wasn't easy, but if I hadn't
been there Dad would've died sooner and

Billy would've been in care. I was old enough to take care of them all so I did."

"And they let you."

"I kinda resented not being able to go out, or date so when I was able to think about travelling, I took the opportunity with both hands. Only I hadn't planned on going alone."

"Meg?"

"It's that obvious?"

"I'd have to walk around deaf, dumb and blind not to notice."

He smiled. "I was going to propose the day I left, take her with me. Fly off into the sunset."

"Romantic."

"It never quite works out the way you think, does it? I never got a chance to propose."

"She announced her pregnancy instead, your brother's kid. Ouch."

"I couldn't think of anything else the entire time I was away. I had the ring ready and an extra plane ticket and this naïve notion the trip would be an engagement present or something. I thought if she knew I still loved her she would give up Billy and come back to me. But they dropped the bombshell about an hour before I left. A couple of times I thought about coming home sooner but then what would've been the point? I thought they were together."

"But they weren't?"

"From what she told me today, far from it." Then he laughed.

"What's so funny?"

"You."

"Me?"

"Yeah, I don't talk to people much. I certainly don't go tellin' them my life story the first day I meet 'em! And here I am talkin' to you like I've known you all my life. "I miss talking to my mom. This is the next best thing, I reckon."

"Thank you, honey. That'll be the trainin'."

"So, you're counselling me?"

"You think you need it?"

"I don't know what I need."

"I think I do. But you are a little young and I reckon I'd eat you for breakfast," she winked.

He laughed. It felt good and was good to see.

"You know what I think, about the Meg and Billy situation?"

"What?"

"I think you should give it a couple of weeks, let the news of your father sink in and then talk to them both."

Oddly, he'd almost forgotten about Hank's death. Just by spending time talking with Sal, she'd made him feel better. Being with someone who wanted to help him rather than have his help, draining him mentally and emotionally, meant the world.

"What would I say?"

"Ask them what they want. You never know, they might not be good together with a baby as well and then you could step in as needed. On the other hand, if they're meant to be together you'll have to accept it."

"I think seeing Meg all over Billy at the hospital told me what I needed to know."

"Don't take that to heart, honey. She's just as upset over Hank as you both are. She's been livin' with him, right?" Garrett nodded. "It's goin' to hit her hard too. She came to the hospital, didn't she? She didn't have to."

"But she went straight to him."

"Is that what this is about? I saw that smile she gave you, it was important. She was asking your permission to comfort Billy. I think I know who she wants to be with and it ain't your brother."

"But he's LJ's father."

"You know that for sure?"

"Yeah. We never slept together, we were together for just three months."

She grinned enthusiastically. "That tells me everything I need to know. She's definitely in love with you. She's with Billy out of loyalty. And I think she's only doing that to please you."

"How can you know that for sure?"

"In the three months you dated you didn't try to sleep with her. You're a perfect gentleman. There ain't many guys like you in the world."

"Don't get me wrong, we got close but we stopped before. I love her. I knew that from the day we started dating. I wanted to be her husband but there's a few years between us. I didn't want to force her to do something she wasn't ready for. Anyway, ever since I've been back all I've done is force the two of them together and barkin' at Billy to get a job so he can support her and the baby."

"Has he got one yet?"

"I got him one this morning. But he says he ain't going."

"It seems you've done everything in your power to fix their problems for them."

"If I'd known how it was for her while I was away, I'd have come back sooner. In a heartbeat."

"I don't doubt it. But now it all appears to be fixed, what is there left for you to do?"

"I start at my old job on Monday. Who knows, maybe we'll sell the ranch and find another place to live."

"And in the meantime?"

"What?"

"What happens if they don't want to be together?"

"I'll be there to pick up the pieces, if she wants me."

"She's a lucky girl. She can't put a foot wrong. But she left you once before, it doesn't worry you she could be tempted again?"

"Billy can be pretty scheming when he wants to be. It wasn't her fault. I was distracted and he wanted to hurt me."

"Which he did."

"Yeah. I can't forgive him."

"But you can forgive her?"

"Sure."

"But does she deserve your forgiveness?"

Garrett sipped his coffee and thought for a moment. "Billy can be conniving and manipulative when he wants something. He wanted to hurt me, I was working late savin' for the trip. I didn't think for a moment she'd fall for his ways but," he shrugged. "I guess she did. I'd been working fourteen-hour days; I couldn't think straight and seeing them together was more than I could take. The next time I saw her was on Billy's arm, I didn't say a word, not one. I didn't even fight for her."

"Why didn't you?"

"I guess I just accepted that she didn't want me anymore. Billy doesn't even care about either of them. LJ's this beautiful little thing. Beats me how she's half his. Meg told me he hasn't even held her. That ain't natural?"

Sal shook her head. "Doesn't sound right to me at all. They're together for all the wrong reasons. Would you step up again and be a husband and father?"

"Sal, hand on heart, I'd do it in a heartbeat."

She laughed. "Yeah, I think you would. There ain't many men who'd do what you've done and ever fewer who'd pick up the pieces afterwards. Does Meg know you're still in love with her?"

"If she has even half a brain…"

"Seems to me if you love her and little LJ that much, you'd be a good surrogate father if your brother didn't stick around. Kevin grew up without a daddy and a lot of times it was real hard. A kid needs a father figure around."

"Did Kevin ever ask you about his father?"

"Yeah. We got into a lot of fights over that one."

"What did you tell him?"

"The truth, makes no sense shrouding it in mystery. Kids need to know who they are even if the sons-of-bitches-fathers don't hang around to watch them grow up."

"How did he take it?"

"Like any other twelve-year-old kid. He kicked the apartment walls until they had holes in them, smashed all the windows in a house down the street and run away for three days. But it made him a better father to Joshua." She glanced at the clock and smiled. "You better get yourself some sleep. You've had the day from hell but it'll feel better in the morning."

That wasn't going to be difficult. The more he thought about his bed, the more he realised how much he needed to be in it. Jet lag had finally taken him. He left Sal's place, got in his truck and drove back home. By now Meg, Billy and little LJ would be sound asleep. All he had to do was stay awake long enough to get home.

Chapter Nine

When Garrett arrived, the lights inside the house were still on. He hoped that meant someone had left them on for him and not that they were still awake.

Meg sat on the couch in her white cotton nightdress with LJ asleep in her arms.

"I've just got her off to sleep," she whispered. Fatigue laced her voice. "Please don't go yellin', okay?"

"Yellin' about what?" he asked quietly. She shook her head but didn't volunteer any information. He looked down the hallway past his father's bedroom and thumbed at Billy's room. "He asleep? I'll go check."

"Garrett, there's no point." She hadn't finished. "Like I said, don't go yellin'."

"What's goin' on?"

"Billy's gone."

"Gone where?"

"Left."

He sat down opposite and rested his head in his hands. He badly needed a shower, not to mention a shave and a change of clothing but more than that he needed sleep. He leaned back on the couch, let his head hang backwards and sighed.

"You're not yellin'?" she whispered.

"You asked me not to."

"Aren't you goin' to say anythin'?"

He looked at her, shrugged and shook his head. "What'd be the point?"

"He said he needed space, there was nothin' malicious about his leavin'. In fact, it felt like it was the right thing for him to do under the circumstances."

"Under the circumstances? You mean the fact that he's a total loser and can't be there for anybody but himself?"

"I mean that his father died tonight."

"My father died too, Meg," he growled, "but you don't see me usin' that as an excuse to go runnin' off at the first opportunity, do you?"

"It's harder for him. He still hasn't grown up, Garrett."

He shrugged. "Billy knows only one way – his way or no way. He doesn't respect anyone. You just can't build a life like that. He was already packed. He was goin' anyway whether Dad died or not."

"Garrett!"

"It's the truth. He told me. That's why we got into a fight earlier."

She looked away disgusted, as if he was lying.

"What? You don't believe me? Everybody in the bar heard him say it. Hell, they even stopped to listen. We were the Friday night cabaret." His voice gained volume with every word.

"You'll wake her. What time is it?"

"A little after one. You should go to bed. There's nothin' to stay up for now. Billy ain't coming back and Dad sure as hell ain't."

"She'll be out of routine now," she sighed, ignoring him. "I was just getting settled into one as well."

She pulled herself to the end of the couch and stood. Garrett stood in front, ready to assist.

"If she cries in the night, I can take care of her if you like."

"She'll be fine," she said curtly. "I don't need any help."

"Meg, what's wrong?"

"Nothin'."

He watched her walk down the hall and kick the bedroom door closed behind her. Whatever he'd said or done was beyond him and right now he was too tired to even contemplate thinking about it any longer. He turned off the den light, walked past his father's room and touched the closed door.

"Night, Dad."

Then, past Billy's room, he shook his head. Finally at the end of the hallway Meg's closed door told him explicitly she didn't want any visitors. He walked inside his room and closed the door quietly behind him. Within seconds he was asleep.

When he awoke the next morning, it wasn't to the sound of the Morning Chorus as he did the previous day, this time it was to the sound of LJ screaming her head off and the cries resonated through the entire house. Garrett pulled back the sheets and pulled on his jeans and made his way to the kitchen.

Scraping his hair back, he scratched his scalp and yawned while he looked through the kitchen window. A glorious day looked back at him. He'd sure missed this weather in Europe, spending Christmas in London was amazing –

but wet, dark and dull. He filled a glass tumbler with water, downed it and refilled it downing that one just as quickly.

He wondered why LJ was still screaming. Surely Meg couldn't sleep though that noise.

"Meg?" he knocked on the door, first softly then, when there was little chance of anybody hearing him above the noise, again louder. "You okay?" He pushed open the door to see LJ lying in her crib as red as a beetroot. "Hey little one, are you hungry? Where's your mommy?"

He held her close, gently cupping her head and took her to the kitchen. From the smell of her, her upset wasn't just through hunger alone. He'd seen bottles prepared enough times to know what he should do: change LJ while the formula prepared. Looking through the refrigerator for a pre-prepared one, he rocked the infant to ease her upset but she wasn't a patient baby. The louder her screams got the deafer Garrett became. He boiled the kettle, stood the bottle in a glass bowl and waited for it to warm.

"Come on, it ain't that bad," he smiled at her, making faces. LJ cried real tears. This wasn't just hunger, she was mad at the stench from her diaper. "Okay, I get it. I'll get you changed, fed and then hopefully your mommy will be back."

He took her back to Meg's room searching for diapers. An opened pack stood at the rear of her bed along with a box of wipes, cream and diaper disposable sacks. He hadn't changed a baby since Billy was born but laid her down, got down on his knees and offered her a friendly smile.

"You're goin' to have to help me out a little here, sweetheart. I ain't done this for a very long time. She kicked her chubby legs out at him and made him smile. LJ quietened down almost immediately but she was still hungry. Garrett changed her, applied cream and gave her a new diaper before lifting her to his bare chest.

"There, see?" he told her authoritatively, settling her in his arms. "This is easy. Let's get some breakfast inside you and before you know it your mommy will be back. Do you know where she went?"

LJ stared at him.

When he reached the kitchen, the formula was ready. He took it out of the bowl, wiped it dry and tested it on his wrist. He held the bottle to her mouth and she sucked it greedily. The skin on her back lay against his open palm. It was satin soft and as warm as a kitten. He turned to the door to see Meg watching them both silently.

"Where were you?" Garrett asked. "She was cryin'. I had to change her."

"I couldn't sleep so I thought I would go look for Billy. I thought I knew where he might have gone."

"He's long gone," he said looking back down at LJ. "Where did you look?"

"All over. I borrowed your truck. I hope that was okay. I didn't want to wake you. I thought she'd sleep longer. She's getting herself into a different routine now. I guess it was too much to ask for her to stay in the other one."

"A lot happened last night. Babies pick up on everything."

"Don't presume to tell me about my baby, Garrett. I know how to care for her."

"I wasn't suggesting you didn't. No point in askin' how you are today."

"I'm fine." It was obvious too little sleep and the mess Billy created wasn't doing her any good. She stepped forward to take her baby.

"It's okay, I've got her. We're doin' fine here," he said.

"She's my child, Garrett. I don't need you to take care of her."

"I beg to differ. She was yellin' her little tiny head off and you weren't anywhere to be seen so I'd say you needed someone then, wouldn't you agree?" He tried to sound friendly but it came out smugly.

"I'm sorry, it won't happen again." She tried again to take LJ but Garrett pulled back.

"I said we're doin' okay. Why don't you take advantage of the fact and go do something for yourself. I'm bettin' Billy didn't give you time alone like that."

"Well, he's not goin' to now, is he?"

"That was his choice. Nobody forced him go do something stupid, did they?"

"Didn't they?" she asked, her eyebrow arching.

Garrett looked up and saw her glaring at him, waiting for an answer.

"What? You think I drove him out of here?"

"You were on his back from the moment you got home."

"Come on, Meg. I got him to face up to his responsibilities."

"Oh, you sure got him to do that. And now he's gone."

"I think you're mad at the wrong brother."

"This might come as a shock to you but we were actually doing okay before you came back. Billy may not have helped out much but at least I knew where he was. Now I don't even have a clue."

He was stunned. Meg was actually defending Billy, again.

"Well, Megan, this might come as a shock to *you* but the first place a father should be is with his family not proppin' up a bar some place. Billy and I both went through that when we were kids. All I was doin' was teachin' him how to provide for his family."

"We would have been fine, Garrett. He got a job, remember? As soon as he'd worked a few weeks, he'd have been right back on track. I know he would."

"*I* got him that job. You might want to remember that before you go thinking bad of me."

Meg's chin wobbled and her eyes filled up. A moment later she was running down the hallway and into her room, slamming the door behind her.

He looked down at LJ. "That went well."

Twenty minutes went by before he attempted to knock on her door. LJ was asleep again in his arms and he wanted to put her down. He held the baby in one arm and knocked gently on Meg's door with the other one.

"Meg. I'm sorry."

"Go away." From her tone, she was done crying. Now she was just mad.

"I need to put her down. Can I at least come in and do that?"

He heard shuffling from the other side of the door and suddenly it opened. She quickly took LJ from him and closed the door again in his face.

"That ain't very friendly." He turned the handle and let the door open. She was putting LJ back into her crib. "Can I come in please?"

"Why?"

"Because you're upset and I don't want you to be."

"Why does it matter to you whether I'm upset?"

"It matters a great deal, Meg. You know it does. I care about you."

She turned to face him. Her tears had gone but her face was blotchy where she'd been crying.

"Well, it needn't matter to you any longer," she said, "because I've made a decision."

"What's that?"

"When I was out earlier, I saw Carla Henry and we talked. LJ and I are going to stay with them until I get myself sorted."

"What?" Garrett almost doubled up as if he'd suffered a blow in the gut as he absorbed the news.

She pulled her case from under the bed and threw it on the bed.

"We're leaving."

Chapter Ten

"You can't leave," he barked. "I won't let you!"

"Who do you think you are, Garrett Cobb? You don't own me."

Instantly LJ woke up and started crying again.

"Why the hell would you want to leave? What the hell is wrong with you?"

"There's nothin' wrong with *me*," she yelled. "I'm perfectly fine. Close the door on your way out."

"Meg, come on, this is your home." His impatience subsiding, he extended a compassionate arm. "Is this your hormones speaking? Mum had it with Billy. I get it. It's not easy." He remembered his mother's mood swings and, at the time, thought it was something he'd done or the fact that Hank was always out drinking. Finally, at school, a teacher explained.

Meg faced him. Her eyes grew large with frustration.

"What do you know about hormones? Nothin'. You know nothin' about what I've been through. You think you can fix all this but really you're just creatin' problem after problem. All I wanted was to have a perfect little family but you've ruined everythin'."

"What did I do?"

"You worked late, you left Maynard and worse than anything, Garrett Cobb, you never fought for me."

He tried to comfort her but again she pushed him away. "Where's all this comin' from?"

She picked up a spare bottle from LJ's supply and pulled it back over her shoulder ready to launch it in his direction.

"Okay, okay, I get it. I'm out of here." He backed out of the room and closed the door. As it clicked shut, the plastic bottle hit it and fell to the floor.

He'd give her some time to re-think her plans. She wasn't going anywhere and neither was LJ if he had anything to do with it. He thought about getting showered and shaved before any more Meg-related events occurred. He glanced at the kitchen clock. It was almost eleven. He hadn't realised how jet-lagged he'd been but a shower would rectify things.

He opened the bathroom cabinet and took out his toothbrush and brushed his teeth. He turned on the shower, rejoicing in the feeling the water brought and afterwards, he left the bathroom with just a towel around his waist. Meg's door was open, clearly not an invitation but he took it as less of a barrier. He stopped just outside to listen for any clues as to her frame of mind.

"You okay?" he stood cautiously back from the door, he didn't want anything else thrown at him. There was no answer. He pushed it open a little more but neither Meg nor LJ were inside. A feeling of dread swept through his gut. When she said she was leaving, surely she didn't mean right at that moment. He ran down the hallway, opened up

the front door and went outside hoping she
hadn't left in the five minutes he'd been
showering. A sense of partial relief grew in his
stomach when he saw his truck was still there.
She hadn't gone.

Meg looked up from the blanket on the
ground next to the swing set. LJ was lying on
it, gurgling and fidgeting.

"Shouldn't you get dressed?"

The swing set chair was in need of an
upgrade with evidence of rust at the base on
the grass. It wasn't the only thing that had
been neglected while Garrett had been
travelling.

The scent of budding spring flowers and
shrubs filled his nostrils but the off-white
picket fence Billy had crashed into a hundred
times caught his attention more; it needed
repainting. Though it stood erect around the
perimeter of the garden, it looked tired and
worn. He'd get around to it now he was home,
that and a thousand other jobs.

"I thought you'd gone," he said holding
the towel around his waist.

Water droplets were still evident on his
legs, clutching at his dark hairs. His chest and
muscular torso sparkled, warranting a second
look while broad shoulders and biceps almost
seduced her there and then. Why she fell for a
one-night-stand with Billy when she was still
so attracted to Garrett confused her.

Suddenly she was very aware of staring at
him.

"Fine. I'm…er…sorry for the outburst
earlier. You were right about the hormone

thing. Carla said she had mood swings after she had Tommy."

"Mom had it with Billy, but he always did bring out the worst in people." Before he realised his words, he apologised. "Sorry, Meg. I guess it's just too easy to direct my anger at him. He's always been useless."

"But he's LJ's daddy," she said as if he needed reminding. "You don't want her growing up thinking of him as a loser. When she's older, if that's all she ever hears from you, she'll believe it. He's got a lot of goodness to give, Garrett, if you would only give him a chance."

"But that's all everybody ever does. That's the problem. He takes every chance he's given and throws it all away. He's always been the same."

"I wish you could see what I see."

"You're alone with that, Meg. He's just a born loser," he shrugged. "I guess he took after Dad."

She didn't respond. LJ kicked her legs in the air as if she were trying to stretch her tiny socks through her cotton dress.

"But I'm glad you've finally realised he's gone for good," he went on. "He ain't coming back."

"He'll be back some day."

"Maybe."

"Carla said they'll put us up for a while. Chris doesn't mind and Tommy will have LJ to play with until he gets bored."

Garrett walked out to her. "You know this really isn't necessary. Hell, I'm not thrilled about this whole situation but I'll be goddamned if I'll let you go live some place else. You both belong here."

"We're not your—"

"How many times are you going to throw that at me, huh? LJ may not be mine, but you're both more mine than the Henry's. You're part of my family and I'm losing family members by the minute right now. You're part of the Cobb family and whether you like it or not, the fact still remains."

"Despite everything, I am happy about it. He's very young inside, Billy I mean. He's very immature and that's why I think he needs taking care of. Aren't you worried something might happen to him now he's alone? He doesn't have much money and I don't know what he packed."

"He'll get by. He needs to do a hell of a lot of growing up and soul-searching. Maybe this is the only way he can do it."

"You'd better get dressed," she said quietly. "You don't want anyone drivin' by and seeing you half naked with your brother's girl."

"People can think what they want to think. I've never given a lot of thought to it, if I did, I don't know how I would've coped with my dad."

"You don't think when people hear that Billy's gone that they'll wonder what I'm doing still living here…with his brother?"

"Does it matter?"

"It matters to me."

"It's nobody's business but ours."

"People make it their business, Garrett. That's what life is like in Maynard. Don't you remember or did your trip make you forget life around here?"

"I remember. But listen to me," he said, "all that matters is that you and LJ are living in a good home where you have family who care for you and love you both."

"Why are you being so good to me?" She stared up at him, tears in her eyes. "I walked out on you for him. How can you take me into your home and care for his baby after everything I put you through?"

"Because it's still important to me that you're cared for. Why don't you just sit tight for a while? There's no need for any hasty decisions. I'm back at work on the construction site Monday and I could sure use some help around the place while I'm out. It sure will be quiet all alone."

"I don't know, Garrett. I just don't know."

"You know it's funny. When I was away, all I could think about was coming home and seeing you and now I'm back all you want to do is leave."

"I just think it will be better if we go."

"You know I keep thinking if I hadn't been working late that night then none of this would have happened. You said before that I ruined everything. How?"

"You left for Europe."

"You left me first, Meg." He didn't want to say those words but he had no choice.

"You were spendin' all your time workin' and savin' for your trip and I hardly got a look in. I barely saw you."

"But I had a ticket for you too," he urged. "I didn't plan on goin' alone. I was going to take you with me."

"You left that part out until it was too late. I didn't think you wanted me anymore."

"Is that why you went with my brother?"

"I needed to feel wanted. To be loved."

"I loved you, Meg. I always did. I've never stopped."

She stood from the blanket. He watched her walk over to him until they were so close she was almost touching his body. With nothing but a towel separating her from his flesh, he swallowed hard.

"And now?"

"You know how I feel. I can't hide it. I never could with you. I love you more now than I ever did," he said softly. He leaned down and kissed her lips gently. Then taking her face in his hands, he deepened the kiss, wanting her more with every moment.

Suddenly she broke the embrace, straightened her clothing and looked around as if expecting cars filled with Maynard residents to zoom past.

"I'll make you a deal."

"Go on."

"I'll postpone going to Carla's until after the funeral. You're gonna need the support. But just until the funeral," she stressed. "Afterwards, we're gone."

Chapter Eleven

The days leading up to the funeral were bleak. Burying his father was one thing but knowing the love of his life was taking her baby and leaving right afterwards was a kick in the gut.

Throwing himself into the new job was a blessing. The new shopping mall was going to be the next big thing for Maynard. Garrett and his crew were sent to construct a warehouse frame. He was happy to get back to it, it was something else to focus on. Creating was everything and provided a welcome change from saying goodbye to family members. Travelling was good fun but creating something out of nothing with his bare hands was good, honest labour. It felt refreshing and worthwhile and felt like a million miles away from fighting with his brother every moment of the day.

By ten, perspiration patches under his arms and down his chest stood out as if the pattern on his light grey T-shirt was deliberately darker. By midday, he needed a break.

"Cobb?" Tony shouted from the other side of the site.

"Be right there."

Meg had shown up and Tony left them together. The brief thought that Billy might have returned flew across his mind as the funeral was imminent, but he knew Billy wasn't going to show up for that.

He took off his hard hat and placed it on Meg's head.

"I brought you this." She handed him a brown bag with sandwiches inside, an apple and a bottle of water.

"Thank you. It looks good on you, keep it on while you're here. We should get one for LJ." He smirked. "Where is she anyhow."

"In the car with Carla and Tommy. We're taking the kids to the park."

"Sounds like fun."

"LJ will probably sleep all through it but Tommy will enjoy it, I'm sure."

Garrett looked over his shoulder and spotted Carla's car, waved, and received a smile in return.

"She gave me a ride to the store," Meg said. "I thought I should get a few things in for tomorrow. People will need to eat."

"Right. Of course. Thanks, I appreciate it. I guess I've been trying to put it out of my mind. I don't think I would've thought about food until after the funeral."

"Well, it would've been a little late by then."

"Yeah." Garrett stared ahead, despite wanting to look at her but something stopped him. The small talk felt forced, awkward, and most of their conversations related to LJ or Billy nowadays anyway. "Though I don't know why people need feeding after a thing like that. It's usually the last thing on my mind."

"It's expected. It's looking good out here. It looks like something is starting."

"Works progressing. Takes a while. Be good when it's done."

"I still can't believe Hank's gone," she said softly. "I still expect him to be there. I mean, I know I didn't see a lot of him but I still cleaned up after him. There's just nothing to clean up now."

"I don't think it's completely sunk in yet. It'll take a little while."

She tried to be casual, considerate. "How are you holding up?" He didn't respond, he just waved away the question. "You think Billy will show?" He shook his head. "I knew you'd say that."

He inhaled and let out a choked cough. "I'm not even sure Billy realises Dad's gone."

"But it's his father's funeral, surely he'd come back for that."

Finally, he turned to face her. "All I'm sayin' is don't go lookin' out for him in the morning. Disappointment is a horrible thing and it'll already be a horrible day." He cupped her chin. "And I don't want you feelin' like that all day." Garrett glanced at his colleagues from a distance. Some had stopped working, staring at them both, waiting for something interesting to happen, something to gossip about and take home to their wives for them to gossip about with each other. "Looks like we got ourselves an audience."

"I didn't mean to embarrass you."

"You couldn't possibly embarrass me, Meg. They're looking 'cause you're so beautiful."

She smirked away his compliment. "They're looking for something juicy to report back to their wives."

"Then maybe we shouldn't disappoint them."

"Garrett!" She gasped then laughed, pulling her arms across her chest. "Anyway I hope the sandwiches are okay."

Garrett looked at them. "I'll have somethin' to say, if they don't quit staring real soon."

"I wish they'd stop looking. I don't know what they think's gonna happen."

"That's it." He tilted his head hard at them ordering them back to work. They complied instantly.

"They listen to you, that is impressive."

"Their regular boss is out so today it's me."

Meg smiled. "I might have said something to Carla."

"Excuse me?"

"About how good you'd be working for her dad. Maybe she said something?"

Garrett grinned. "Well, that was pretty sneaky. Thank you."

"A little help doesn't hurt, does it?" she smiled. "I thought it was time to reciprocate. I'd better get back."

The gesture surprised him. It felt strange to have someone look out for him.

"Give LJ a hug from me." Without thought, he leant forward and kissed her as a loud cheer, whooping and laughing came from the direction of his co-workers. Garrett saw money changing hands among them.

But he couldn't have cared less.
***

Inside the park, Carla put down a large patchwork blanket. It was big enough for their picnic, the kids and the two women to sit on. Tommy played next to it with a ball and Carla played with him while Meg dished up the food.

Tommy tried to kick the ball and missed it several times before he fell over. As Carla bent over to support Tommy by his underarms she lifted him up off the grass and brought him down quickly to kick the ball. Her blonde bobbed hair hung down over her forehead. Tucking it behind her ears, she laughed.

"There you go, little guy. Chris kicks a ball in the yard with him all the time but I often wonder who that's really for."

"They're all big kids at heart," Meg agreed, laying cheese sandwiches on a plastic plate for Tommy. "LJ's not a month old yet and Garrett still plays with her every night. I don't think he'd be at all surprised if she suddenly got up off the floor and asked him to play ball."

Carla brought Tommy back to the blanket to eat. She tore off some of the cheese sandwich and gave it to him.

"It does sound like things have settled down for you now. I've gotta be honest, he sounds pretty amazing."

Coyness covered Meg's face. "What are you saying?"

"Nothing, I just think you have yourself a pretty good set up considering how things were a few weeks ago."

"You know there's nothing going on between us."

"But you've got to admit, he's a sexy guy and a great catch."

"I guess."

"You guess?"

"Well," she grinned. "Yeah, he is pretty amazing."

Carla shoved a piece of Tommy's sandwich in her mouth. "He's got an amazing body, I mean, if I wasn't with Chris…" Meg giggled at her. "Well, I would. He's gorgeous."

"I didn't expect to hear you say that. You're a married woman."

"Married, not dead. I'm also not blind, the guy is a living god. You'd be dumb not to check him out. I'm not alone either. Sal, from the diner, talks about him all the time. She's like his own private fan club. She doesn't seem to care what others think either. Power to her. I'd love to be like that."

"And yet she chose to live here, the gossip town of Texas."

"Everyone seems to have a crush on your boyfriend."

"He ain't my boyfriend," she said firmly. "He hasn't been for some time."

"You've been the talk of the town for at least a week, Meg. It's gonna happen, I mean they had all-out fights in the middle of bars. Everyone heard their private business. And those who didn't hear it first-hand, heard about it the next day." She gave Tommy another piece of sandwich which he took happily whilst playing with a toy truck on the blanket. "I have to admit, I knew they were trouble but I hadn't realised there was more to it than how it looked on the surface."

Meg turned over onto her stomach resting her chin on her hands.

"I think it's wrong for people to talk about the Cobb brothers. They're a good family. I remember seeing Laura when I was a kid at school with Billy. She was a real nice lady. But people only see what they want to see. They don't know that Hank drunk himself to death with guilt, or that Garrett raised Billy, they just saw three guys fighting. It's really sad. I guess it's easier to see the bad in people than the good."

"I never knew Laura. My father-in-law used to work as a ranch hand with Hank when they were younger. He never holds back if he thinks someone is a bad egg, so I guess I heard it from him. That's gotta be tough though, hearing folk talking about your dead mom. And now Hank's gone. And Billy. You're right, it's sad."

"Yeah, nothing's been easy for months."

"You know if I was in your situation and my boyfriend walked out on me, and suddenly his brother – my ex – wanted to step in, I'd seriously consider it. I mean what have you got to lose."

"What are you saying? You don't want me to stay at yours?" she asked.

"No, silly, I'd love you to stay with us but I just don't see why you'd want to. You've got everything you need there, it's a huge family home with a guy who's falling over himself to make life even better for you. He's employed. He's single. He's got morals. He's a freaking god. I just don't get it."

"Like I said, it isn't like that between us."

"I saw him kiss you earlier. I think he wants it to be like that."

"He does," Meg told her, frankly. "That's just the problem. It's obvious how he feels about me."

"Has he told you he loves you?"

Meg nodded.

"You know some women spend their whole lives looking for a guy like Garrett Cobb and you're already *living* with him!"

"I'm not living with him, we just happen to be in the same house together." She saw the glint in Carla's eye.

"Don't you like him anymore?"

"I don't know."

"How can you not know? There's either chemistry there or there isn't."

"Oh, there's chemistry all right," Meg nodded. "But I slept with his brother, Carla. I can't pretend that didn't happen."

"Honey, I think he forgives you."

"It's not as easy as that. I don't think I can forgive myself."

Chapter Twelve

Standing at the side of the casket with friends
and townsfolk who knew the truth about the
family, Garrett and Meg were silent. The priest
said his words and Hank was lowered into the
ground. It was a simple but emotional
ceremony.

Of the twenty people who made the effort
to show up, Hank's youngest son wasn't one
of them. Garrett had stopped looking for him
fifteen minutes ago.

At the corner of his eyes, he saw Megan
wipe away tears. His hand sought hers and
they linked fingers. Each hand brought cold
with them and created heat after a few
seconds. The connection was necessary, he
didn't care who saw it. When he did steal a
glance, she looked pale. Her brunette hair was
twisted behind her head and fastened with a
silver clip and the white shirt she wore was a
stark contrast to the borrowed-from-Carla
black trousers. She looked elegant, and Hank,
in his sober hours – which were few – would
have been proud.

Garrett, looking forward again, watched
the casket reach its destination and choked.
His mother's funeral was the last and only
other he'd attended; almost a
hundred people paid their respects. Compared
to the gathering today, Laura had been treated
as the local treasure she was. He thought about
them together again. They were such different
people, and he wondered, with an adult mind,
what she'd seen in him. She rarely drank, was

open and friendly and took enormous pleasure in raising her sons. Even with Hank less in the picture as time moved on, she adored and worshipped her boys.

Sal stepped forward as the attendees drifted apart.

"Honey, I'm so sorry," she kissed his cheek and wiped her lipstick from it.

"Thanks for being here," he smiled politely. "Maybe you'd like to come back to the house with everyone else?"

"Thank you."

He watched her walk towards Dirk, Chris and Dan for her ride back.

"Meg, would you mind going back with someone else? I want to spend some time with my mama. I won't be long."

"I can stay. Carla can let everyone in."

He shook his head. "I'd rather be alone."

She left him, looking back one more time. Slowly the crowd dispersed and before long Garrett was standing alone facing his mother's grave. He stood, passing the rim of his Stetson through his hands.

"Mom, I needed to talk, sorry I haven't been back here in a while. I've been away, you know how it is. It's been tough since you left. I did the best I could but he ain't here today, I don't know why. What am I supposed to do? I can't fix it all the time, he sabotages everything. He resents me for raising him, like it made him different from the other kids. He used to say he was confused, was I his brother or his mama or his dad. How do you answer that? I was all those things. I was still growing up too." He sobbed, "I did my best. And now there's Meg. I can give her everything she needs but she won't take it. I love that baby like she's my own, I can't let her leave me. I can't take one more person leaving me. I need her, I'm lost without her." Tears streamed down his face. "I miss you, Mom. I miss our chats. We'd talk for hours. You always did know what to say for the best, fixing things for me. Well, I guess it's up to me now but I don't know if I can fix this problem. Tell me what to do. Please."

If there were any voices to be heard from beyond the grave, Garrett didn't catch any evidence. "I guess I'd better go, there'll be people waiting at the house. I can't leave Meg to face them all alone. Bye, Mom." He put on his Stetson and doffed it at her grave. "I love you."

Meg opened the door to him. She could see from his bloodshot eyes that he'd been crying. He didn't speak and nor did she.

An hour later, people began to leave. Once one went, others followed and pretty soon the house was almost empty apart from Chris. Tommy sat on his lap playing with one of LJ's furry toys.

"I hate these things but thanks for coming, man," Garrett hugged Chris. "It means a lot."

"Last one I went to was your mama's. They're tough. You just gotta get through the day. I'm sorry about Billy, man."

"Yeah. It's not like you can hide that kinda thing, is it?"

"I think everyone's on your side, if that helps any."

It didn't, it just reinforced the idea that the town was still gossiping about the Cobb boys.

"Thanks. I'm gonna check on Meg." He knocked on her bedroom door and waited. It sounded like Carla was with her.

"Meg, can I come in?"

"She's changing LJ," Carla told him. "I'll leave you two alone."

He peered over Carla's shoulder and saw a suitcase on the bed next to LJ. She was still going through with it.

"Seriously, can't you wait just one more day. Don't do this today of all days. Please."

"I told you I'd stay as long as the funeral."

He pushed the door closed behind him and stood facing her.

"Why the hell are you doing this? I need you."

"I have no choice." She pushed him aside. The mere touch of his solid body forced her into reconsidering but it was no use. Her mind had been made up.

"You have plenty of choices. Stay. I can't live in this place all by myself. I just can't do it."

"You'll be fine. You'll meet someone."

"What? I'm not interested in anybody else. I want you."

"Stop it," she said, her eyes tearing up. "They'll hear us."

"What is it? You want me to beg, is that it? Fine, I'll beg."

"Leave me alone. I can't live here."

"Why not? I love you."

She pushed him against the door so hard, LJ stopped gurgling in her crib and seemed to be watching them.

"That's why not."

"*Because* I love you? I can't help it," he admitted. "I've never stopped."

"And I've never stopped loving you either," she cried, "but that doesn't matter anymore."

"If you love me, Meg, why won't you stay? We can make a life here together, the three of us."

She struggled down the hallway until Carla took LJ from her.

"Meg, wait," Garrett called.

"I'm sorry. I never meant it to be this hard."

Garrett's eyes blurred with tears. "Jesus Christ! Don't leave me. Not again."

But it was no use. Meg was gone.

Chapter Thirteen

"Man! You've got to get her to talk to me," Garrett howled down the phone to Chris Henry. "She's not thinkin' straight. Let me talk to her, Chris. *Please.*"

"I'm sorry, there's nothing I can do. She doesn't want to speak to you."

"I promise, I won't take long."

"Garrett, calm down, give it a couple of days. Just to cool off."

"Chris, you don't understand—"

"Garrett," he shouted, "get some rest. She's safe here, you know that but if there's one piece of advice I can give you is that women never do something they don't want to. Let her think things through for a couple of days."

Maybe Chris was right, she just needed some space. That was fine, he'd give it to her. He'd give her the world if she asked for it.

He needed to keep busy. The silence was deafening and teacups littered the table. Paper plates punctuated the kitchen with half-eaten sandwiches, and slices of meat courtesy of Sal who brought them from the diner. He sighed, set about clearing up the place throwing all he could in a trash bag and piling the remainder in the kitchen sink. It didn't keep his mind away from her. He recalled the cut on her hand and how they almost kissed.

A half hour later, Meg would be giving LJ her early evening feed, one more before bedtime and she might sleep right through until five in the morning.

He closed his eyes and imagined them
sitting with him.
     * * *
Carla tapped on the bedroom door cautiously.
     "Hey, are you asleep?"
     "No, come on in." Carla stepped inside
and sat on the edge of the bed while Meg fed
LJ. "She's putting on weight real good."
     "She sure is. It's just as well she's too
young to understand anything at the moment.
It's been horrific. He called. Garrett," Carla
nodded apologetically. "Chris told him to give
you some time but I don't think that'll stop
him calling. He's a determined kind of guy."
     "I really appreciate what you're doing for
us, Carla. I shouldn't have put any of you in
this position."
     "That's fine," she squeezed Meg's hand.
"What are friends for?" She watched LJ
sucking the milk. "I think we need to talk. Can
I ask you something? Why are you here?"
     "You want us to leave?"
     "No, I just want to understand it."
     "I'm here because I couldn't be there."
     The look on Carla's face said she was still
confused. "But why?"
     "We talked about this in the park," Meg
explained.
     "Yeah, I remember what you said – or
rather what you didn't say, that you won't
forgive yourself for one stupid night with
Billy Cobb. Big deal, Meg. We all make
mistakes. His big brother certainly forgives
you and the way I see it if anyone should be
dishing out forgiveness, it's him. The thing is,

while Chris and I are happy to help you out, all we're doing really is perpetuating the problem."

Meg stroked LJ's soft hair. "I just can't be with him."

"You feel disloyal somehow?"

"Yeah. To both of them," she let out an odd kind of laugh. "If I stay with Garrett, I'm being disloyal to Billy and LJ but if Billy showed up, where does that leave Garrett?"

"What about what you want?"

"But it's not as easy as that." Her voice was small, like a helpless child in need.

"You love Garrett?"

"Yes, I do."

"But you're scared?"

Meg nodded. "God, I'm so confused. I can't give myself to Garrett completely because LJ doesn't belong to him."

"Do you think he honestly cares about that? From what I've seen he's more than willing to fill that role. Heck, let's face it, he's been a parent since he was twenty."

Meg grinned through tears. "He is pretty perfect, isn't he?"

"I'm looking at a confused woman who's been given the run around by a dead-beat." She stared at LJ and grinned. The baby was almost asleep, her tiny brown eyelashes covered her eyes. "I mean, come on, how many guys would give up something so beautiful. She's adorable for Christ's sake!"

"He never did hold her, you know."

"Not even once?"

Meg shook her head. "He never felt what it's like to hold her close, feel her heart beating, knowing she needs you to survive. Garrett was in the house five minutes and had her in his arms. And you know what? They looked so good together."

"Then why are you in my spare bedroom? You just pack your things and head home in the morning, throw your arms around him and make mad passionate love right there on the floor."

They giggled.

"Give it some thought?"

"I've been thinking of nothing else in days. What if he shows up tomorrow? Five years from now and claims his child? He's her daddy, I can't say no."

"Honey, Billy gave up all rights to his child the moment he abandoned you both. And remember Garrett Cobb is a tough guy. If anybody ever tried to hurt you or her, believe me, he'd be there. Billy didn't show you even the smallest bit of the respect Garrett has. He didn't think twice about letting you go. He couldn't wait to leave town."

"Garrett said that. He told me Billy was set to leave anyway, he just needed a reason and Hank's death was just a convenient excuse."

"Then Garrett's both sexy and smart because it's true. Billy told Dirk that same thing a while ago."

"Why didn't you tell me?"

"Would you have listened?" Carla asked bluntly. "I believe you wanted it to work with Billy just so you could justify leaving Garrett.

You need closure, you need to sit down with Billy and talk this whole thing out."

"That ain't gonna to happen though, is it?"

She put the baby down at the side of her bed and propped her up with a pillow. "She'll be down for hours now."

"Tommy asked me why LJ doesn't play like him. I had to explain she was too little yet." Carla laughed. "That was a learning curve."

"Those damned Cobb brothers have been my undoing from the get-go."

"Without money, he won't have gotten far. I think he's still in town somewhere."

Meg flashed her eyes up. "You do?"

"Can you honestly see him driving out of state? He's got no money, no prospects, he had a job and threw it away. It sounds to me like he might come back, even if it's just to line his pockets to get away properly."

Meg took a deep breath. For the first time in months, she started to feel quietly optimistic.

Chapter Fourteen

Garrett awoke abruptly. The window was open a notch and the net curtain blew softly in the breeze. He looked at the clock, it was almost two in the morning. Three hours or so and LJ would wake Meg for her first feed of the day.

He folded his arm over his eyes.

"Goddamn."

If his mother were still alive, she'd slap him upside the head and give him one of her disapproving glances. He smiled at the thought of her. He missed his mother. And Meg and LJ. And he even missed his father, now he was gone. The house was so quiet without them all filling it. He missed the constant battles with Billy too. At least it removed the silence.

He sighed. If only he'd fought harder for her the first time around there wouldn't have been a second and he may not be lying in his bed alone now.

Coffee. That was a good idea. Coffee and a bagel, *like the ones Meg makes down at the diner*.

"Stop it. Stop torturing yourself."

He swung his legs to the side of the bed and sat there, raking his fingers through his hair. Something outside caught his attention. He held his breath to reduce the noise of his pulse beating in his ears. It happened again, like metal near the front door. Was somebody trying to pick the lock? A key went into the lock and it was turning; he could hear it all from the silence of his room.

Maybe Meg was back. A flutter filled his heart. Oh God, *please* make it be Meg and LJ. He stood in the darkened hallway in his jeans, sparsely lit by the moonlight coming through the kitchen window. The front door opened slowly as a figure stood in the doorway.

"Meg?"

"Bro." Billy was back and he was drunk.

Garrett's heart thumped like a drum. "What the hell do you want?"

"That's a fine way to speak to your kid brother." If his drunken state wasn't bad enough, he'd been in a fight too by the fresh cuts and bruises on his face. They added to the injuries Garrett had inflicted upon him. "I'm back." He laughed, arms outstretched offering a hug. "I came home. I thought you'd be thrilled to see me."

"You've got some nerve showing up like this."

"I live here, don't I?"

Garrett smirked. "No, you don't. You stopped living here when you jumped through the window two weeks ago. In fact, I oughta call the cops and have you arrested for trespassing."

Billy held up his door key. "How can I be trespassing? I have a key."

Garrett nodded to the counter top. "Leave it there and go."

"I ain't going nowhere. I told you, I'm back."

"You must be really stoned, Billy. There ain't no way I'm letting you stay here, not after everything you've done."

"What I do?"

Garrett choked in astonishment. "Have you no conscience at all? You ran out on Meg and LJ and you didn't even have the courtesy to show up for your own father's funeral. That's what you did."

Billy threw his hands up casually, dismissing his brother's comments.

"I can't deal with death, man. You remember how it was when Mom died. I was a mess."

"You can't blame Mom for that. You've always been a mess."

"But I can't handle that kind of thing."

"Right, and I can? 'Cause it's just a walk in the park for everyone else."

"I need a drink."

"You can't keep doing this, Billy. It ain't doing you no good. You'll be dead before you're twenty-five."

He searched through the cupboards above the counter-top and under the sink. "What the hell are you talking about, bro? And where's the liquor?"

Garrett watched him staggering around. Barely out of his teens and Billy was already an old man. It was sad to watch him throw away his life to alcoholism.

"You're sick. You need help."

"Sick of you," he laughed, "yeah."

"No, I mean sick. You're an alcoholic, like Dad was. It's gonna kill you, bro."

"I ain't drunk. And I can give up anytime I choose."

"You just don't choose, yeah I remember how it goes. Please don't make me watch you kill yourself like Dad did. I can't care for you anymore."

Billy stood up and turned, resting his lower back against the edge of the sink.

"You think you know everything, don't you, Garrett. Well, let me explain something to you. I am not your son and I don't have a father or a mother anymore so nobody gets to treat me that way."

"I did my best. Mom died and Dad checked out," he said abruptly. "I had no choice, they might have put you in care."

"Well, look where it got you. I'm him, I'm Dad and you're what? Nobody. You ain't even Mom," he laughed as if the thought tickled him immensely. "And you ain't got a girl so you ain't got no-one. There's nothing for you around here so why don't you go back to Europe and stay there. You've got nothing to keep you here, have you?"

"I hoped I might."

"Well, you don't. Where is she anyhow? And the kid?"

"They left."

"You couldn't keep her twice?" Billy laughed. "Twice you couldn't keep her? Oh, that's the best thing I've heard in ages."

"Watch your mouth."

"Where is she?" he paused for a moment trying to imagine who she would be with. "Well, her mom threw her out so I guess she ain't there. Carla Henry?" he nodded when he saw Garrett's disapproving glare. "Yeah, I'll bet she's staying with them."

"It doesn't matter where they are. What matters is that you stay away from them. They don't need you bothering them anymore and they sure as hell don't need you in their lives."

"No, 'cause the magnificent Garrett Cobb is going to fly in wrapped in his Superhero cape and save the day, just like you always do. She doesn't want you, you know, that's why she came to me in the first place that night."

"She didn't go to you, Billy. Let's get the facts straight here, you lured her from me."

Billy squinted, trying to remember.

"Yeah, that's right. I *lured* her to me. That's a good word, bro. You're clever like that, you always were. So much better than me in every way. You're right we should get it all out in the open and we can all just go on with our lives. I *lured* her to me that night," he said, emphasising the word again. "I knew you were working late, saving your dollars for that trip so you could see the world and better yourself. You left her alone one night too many and I took my chance. She was lonely, did you know that?"

"That's enough."

"Yeah, she was real lonely. So lonely, in fact, that she needed comforting real bad."

"Billy, I'm warning you. Stop it."

"I guess you could say we did a little more than just comfort each other though."

A bad taste formed in Garrett's mouth. If Billy didn't stop very soon, he'd find himself slammed against the floor.

"She said she wanted me too. Did she ever tell you that? Uh-huh, bro, she wanted me. *Me!* Billy Cobb. Suddenly somebody noticed me for a change. Hell, I wasn't going to say no. She's was fine. So I had me a piece of her and, man, was she wild."

Before Billy said any more, Garrett flew through the kitchen and pummelled his brother into the floor. Billy wriggled away before punching Garrett's stomach forcing the wind out of him. He rolled back onto his butt as Billy stood to his feet. Another strike flew into Garrett face, then another.

Billy staggered to his feet and smiled as blood trickled down from his nose. Garrett, for once, looked worse. Lying on the kitchen floor, propped up by the wall, he stared at Billy.

"You see, bro, it ain't always about you either. You know after you left, everybody in town missed you. Hell, any place I showed up you were all they ever talked about. Nobody even saw me. Even after you were gone, you were all they could talk about. Hell, I'm glad I knocked her up, it showed you that I wasn't nothin'. It showed everyone I wasn't nothin'. I could do somethin'."

"But you never even wanted them."

"Hell, no, I still don't. What do I want with a kid in tow?"

"Then why are you here?"

"To pack my bags, I need money."

"You've got to be kidding me. You're despicable, you know that? If I give you money, you'll leave town and never return?"

"You paying me off? Sure, if you make it worth my while."

Garrett had some savings in his room. Something to come back to, he told himself before he left on his travels. It didn't matter if he gave it away, nothing mattered more than getting rid of Billy.

"I've got two thousand. You take it and you go and you never come back. You got it?" Garrett steadied himself by the sink. "And if you ever try to mess with our lives again, Billy, I promise you this. Brother or not, I will kill you."

Chapter Fifteen

It was almost three by the time Billy walked out of the Cobb household forever.

It was as if a huge weight had been lifted. Garrett could breathe easily now and not have to wait for the next problem that needed fixing. He could hardly wait to tell Meg the good news. Two thousand dollars was a small price to pay to rid them all of continual pain and grief.

He headed for his bedroom and got dressed. He wouldn't be able to sleep any more so the sooner he could see Meg to tell her Billy was out of their lives for good, the better, but he'd still have to wait for a more reasonable hour.

He put on a plaid shirt and his jeans and pulled on his boots. He glanced at his face in the bathroom. Billy had swung at him pretty good to create a cut like that on his lip and eye. He wiped it clean weaving his jaw back and forth. Bruising always felt bad and kudos to Billy for landing him a punch like that. He must have picked up moves from bar fights; he'd fought in them often enough.

Garrett splashed water over his face and headed for the kitchen. He needed coffee more now than ever. As he filled up the kettle, the phone rang. At three-twenty in the morning, he knew it wasn't going to be good news. Late night calls never were.

"It's me, Carla," she whispered. "Billy's here and he's real mad. Chris wants you here now. He's trying to quieten him down in case

he wakes up the kids but he won't go until
he's seen Meg and she says she won't see him
while he's drunk. Chris is threatening to call
the cops, Garrett."

"I'm on my way."

He was supposed to leave town, not go to
the Henry's. The kid was a living nightmare.
Within eight minutes Garrett had pulled up
outside; Carla had already opened the door. A
light across the street came on, indicating that
the chaos that followed Billy around was
affecting others too. The town's gossips were
going to get their kicks tonight.

Billy was casually sitting down in the den,
albeit he looked out of place. Chris sat
opposite, standing instantly when he saw
Garrett.

"This is crazy, man," Chris told him,
frankly. "I don't mind looking after your girl
for a few days but I draw the line at visits
from this loser at three-thirty in the morning."

"I'll go make some coffee," Carla said,
hoping to relieve some of the bad feeling.
"Maybe that'll sober him up."

Garrett apologised. "Billy, we had a deal."
He sat forward on the couch opposite, his
arms resting on his thighs. Considering how
their last meeting went, he decided to try the
softly-softly approach. "You and me had an
agreement, didn't we?"

"We did?"

"I gave you some money, remember? You
were supposed to get out of town."

"I wanted to see Meg."

"What would that accomplish?"

"I wanted to see my kid. Nobody can stop me doing that."

"You are a living nightmare, boy. Do you know that?"

"I ain't a boy, I'm a man and I wanna see my kid. I wanna be a daddy now."

That was the last thing Garrett wanted to hear. There was no way he was giving in without a fight. Not this time round.

"Are you saying you want to make things right between you two? That you wanna take care of them? Protect them? Love them? Put their needs before yours?"

Billy looked up. "I'm saying I *think* I want them."

"You *think* you want them?" he repeated, disbelieving his own ears. "Might you only want them because you know I do?"

A hint of a smile crept onto Billy's lips.

"What's stopping you from leaving them again?"

Billy chuckled. "I don't know. I guess you know me better than I know myself."

"I've been fixing your screw-ups your whole life." Carla brought the coffee through on a tray. Garrett took a cup and pushed it into Billy's hands. "Drink this. It'll sober you up."

"I don't wanna be sober. I like drunk."

"Yeah, well we're not here for what you want, Billy. These good people have been disturbed enough by your shenanigans and there's two little kids in the house. There's no need to put anyone through anything more. I'm tellin' you to drink it so drink it."

Obediently, he took the coffee and sipped from the edge.

"Now, we need to sober you up so you and Meg can talk things over 'cause she says she ain't coming down until you are. Which is a perfectly reasonable request, dontcha think?"

Billy looked at Chris and Carla. Neither looked happy.

"Why isn't she here?"

"I just told you. She won't speak to you while you're drunk."

Chris mumbled from the doorway. "Can't say I blame her."

Carla nudged his arm, "Shh!"

"We need to get you sober first," Garrett told him. "Keep drinkin'."

Billy drained the cup and wiped his mouth. "Look, all I want to do is see Meg. Why's everybody makin' such a big deal about it?"

Meg silently entered the room. She folded her arms across her chest, as if to keep out the cold despite wearing a thick towelling dressing gown.

"Because no sane person shows up to talk at three in the morning. I've been listening from upstairs and so far I've not heard anything that makes me want to run your way. You abandoned us. My little girl isn't even a month old and you walked out on us. Have you any idea how that made me feel?"

He shrugged.

"You're enjoying this aren't you, all this attention," she went on. "Do you feel like a big man or something having all these people hangin' on your every word?"

"I feel alright."

Chris gestured he and Carla were heading to the kitchen to give them all privacy.

"I can see you don't think much of anybody but yourself and I feel pretty foolish that I've been loyal to you since that night. So, I only want to know one thing, Billy. Did you ever love me?"

"No. I've never been in love with you. You were wild between the sheets, though."

She ignored the comment. "Well, I loved you. Even if it was just for one night. And you, Garrett," she stared at him, tears in her eyes, "I wanted to hurt you because you weren't there. You'd spent so many nights working late, you didn't even realise I'd gone with your brother. At least, not until you got home that final night."

Garrett walked over to her. He was here for her now.

Billy grinned. "Seems to me everyone got screwed one way or 'nother."

Garrett sneered. "Shut the hell up."

"Or what? You gonna hit me?"

"Stop it, both of you, this is getting us nowhere," Meg hissed.

"Why the hell don't you two kiss and make up? Then you can go get married and make more babies. I don't understand why you haven't done that already."

"Because that little girl upstairs needs her daddy," she reminded him.

"But I don't want a kid, I never did. I keep tellin' you that but you ain't listenin'."

"Billy, keep your voice down."

"Yeah, why what are *you* gonna do if I don't, Megan?"

She slapped his face. It stung too, but he wasn't going to let a girl hit him in front of anyone. He grabbed her arm and slapped her face, forcing her to the couch. Garrett shot across and pushed his brother away.

"Don't you ever touch her again."

"Why the hell do you treat people like this?" she said, holding her jaw. "Do you want LJ to grow up knowing her daddy was nothing but a loser?"

"I never wanted to be a father. As far as I am concerned the kid is yours, not mine. The only reason I went with you was to get at my brother for bein' so damned perfect all the goddamn time."

"Ain't you the least bit sorry?"

"Sorry this whole thing has followed me around like a bad smell? Sure."

"You bastard!" she hissed.

Billy laughed.

"You don't deserve a child and you sure as hell don't deserve my loyalty."

"Well it ain't like I ever asked for it in the first place. I dated girls after being with you, don't you remember?"

Meg raced to the door and opened it. "Get out! I don't want to ever hear from you again. Don't ever try to come back for LJ either because as far as I'm concerned Garrett is her father. You come near us again and I'll call the police and have a restraining order slapped on you."

He casually walked to the door and tapped his pocket. "Thanks, bro." As if possessed by a wave of insanity, instead of leaving the house, Billy rushed to the top of the stairs opening every room door until he found LJ.

Meg shrieked in panic.

"What is it?" Chris yelled from the kitchen.

Meg froze to the floor in terror. "Oh my God, he's going to take LJ!"

Chapter Sixteen

Instantly, Chris called the police as Carla comforted Meg at the bottom of the stairs. Garrett followed his brother, exercising caution.

LJ had been wrenched from the bed and was in Billy's arms. Garrett stood in the doorway watching him. Half of him was ready to grab the baby, the other half ready to tackle his brother.

Chris moved quietly upstairs, guarding Tommy's room with his body. No matter what happened now, his own son wasn't going to be involved in this madness.

"Do not do anything stupid," Garrett pleaded, calmly. "Give her to me and this whole thing will be forgotten."

"Like you're just going to let me walk out of here? I don't think that's going to happen, brother."

"I called the police," Chris whispered behind Garrett. "They're on their way."

"There's no way out of here," Garrett shook his head. "Give her to me."

Billy looked down at the baby in his arms. She was no longer asleep. Instead she opened her eyes and stared at him.

"I'm your daddy," he said. "Makes no difference to me though, I still don't love you and I still don't want you."

"Give her to me."

"You scared I might hurt her? Scared I might drop her?" he over-acted dropping her several times then added, "Throw her down even? What if I did?"

"I'd kill you," he promised. "Then Meg would kill you."

"I've got nothing to lose anyway. Chris called the cops, remember, it's all downhill from here." Billy laughed, inviting the situation.

"Yes, he did. And do you know why? You see, you just can't be this unpredictable. You need specialist help that I can't give you." Somewhere in Garrett's heart, he knew this was what his brother needed: to be arrested and thrown in jail. Keeping on bailing him out of every situation meant he didn't learn but having the police lock him up and the justice system hold him responsible was what he needed. "But it doesn't have to be that bad, Billy, if you just give her to me." He could hear Meg sobbing at the bottom of the stairs and it was breaking his heart. "Can you hear that? Meg's dying inside because of your actions. How can you live with yourself knowing that?"

Billy shrugged. Garrett stepped forward once more and put out his arms.

"I want you to give her to me, now," he said calmly.

In the distance a police siren was getting nearer.

"That's my ride!" Billy giggled, his mind temporarily taken over by insanity. "They're coming for me. I'm going down, aren't I? I'm goin' to jail."

Garrett looked into those chocolate eyes but couldn't see his kid brother inside. "You want them to, don't you?"

Blue flashes illuminated the stairway and a moment later two officers moved up the stairs, weapons cocked.

"Billy, it just got real. Give her to me."

"Bye, bro," he whispered as a tear fell down his cheek. He gently placed the baby into Garrett's arms. Inside the blanket was the roll of dollar bills. He'd returned them. Instantly he was pushed down on his front and cuffed and within minutes he was in the back of the police car while an officer took a statement from each of them.

The sun started to rise, illuminating the Texan sky with its orange blush. Soon, the stars that punctuated the night sky would be just a memory.

Carla hugged Meg. "What will they do with him?"

"They've charged him with attempted abduction, D&D and drink driving and that's just for starters," Garrett told them. "I'm almost certain they'll find somethin' else."

"I don't believe that just happened. It all seems surreal."

"He wanted this. That man there was not the boy I raised, he was gone a long time ago. His eyes, tonight, there was something missing. I've never seen that before. It was terrifying," Garrett confessed. "I've never been so scared."

"Home?" Meg asked.

Garrett gasped. "Yeah. Yeah, absolutely. Come on."

After packing, they said their apologies and goodbyes and were back at the Cobb ranch as the morning light shone.

"I think we should leave LJ to sleep in her own room?"

"She has her own room?" she asked.

"Sure, why not? You want to get some sleep? It's been a pretty tough night."

"Sleep?" she sighed, watching the baby settle. "I don't think I could sleep for hours. I'm somewhere between beat and elated but I don't think I could sleep."

"Good, because there's something I need to say and I need you awake for it."

Meg eyed him suspiciously. "What's going on?"

"I've got nothing to lose and I'm man enough to admit I am terrified I might not get another chance. So, here it is."

He pulled a ring from his jeans pocket. The ring that travelled to Europe and gave him hope that one day it would work its magic. He got down on one knee in front of her.

"Megan, darlin', will you marry me?"

She gasped. "Are you serious?"

"As a heart attack."

"Yes! Yes! Of course, I'll marry you. Yes!"

***

It was a month later that Megan Meyer walked down the aisle in a simple cream dress. At the other end her handsome hero, dressed in a tuxedo, beamed.

LJ sucked her fists inside Carla's arms as Tommy continually asked 'why' to everything in the church that Chris could answer.

Sal stood next to Dirk Henry and his youngest son, Dan, as they listened to the happy couple exchanging vows.

"You may kiss your bride," the Priest announced. The congregation went crazy. Garrett didn't need to be told twice. He leaned in and claimed his bride's lips.

Sal offered the diner for the reception later as white streamers and balloons hung from every window.

"How does it feel to finally be married?" Sal asked them both.

Garrett grinned as Meg choked back her tears of happiness.

"Heavenly," she said.

Garrett kissed her again. "Let's go be a family now, huh?"

About The Author

SJ Banham has been writing for over three decades in diverse genres. She has published fiction, non fiction and ghost written memoirs for private clients. This is her 11th book, which was published after completing her degree, a BA (Hons) in English Literature and Creative Writing. She runs a business, For The Love of Books (www.loveofbooks.co.uk), offering creative writing services including coaching and workshops. She hosts The Versatile Writer podcast.

If you enjoyed this story, she would appreciate your time reviewing it so others may learn about it too.

To follow updates of her work, you can find Sarah on:

Face Book: For The Love of Books
Twitter: @sjbwrites

www.ingramcontent.com/pod-product-compliance
Lightning Source LLC
Chambersburg PA
CBHW070327120726
47909CB00008B/2627